JENNA AITCH

JENNA AITCH

JENNA AITCH IN THE HIGH WATER OF HELL

HOWARD BILLY BURL MCDANIEL

JENNA AITCH
JENNA AITCH IN THE HIGH WATER OF HELL

iUniverse books may be ordered through booksellers or by contacting:

iUniverse
1663 Liberty Drive
Bloomington, IN 47403
www.iuniverse.com
1-800-Authors (1-800-288-4677)

Because of the dynamic nature of the Internet, any web addresses or links contained in this book may have changed since publication and may no longer be valid. The views expressed in this work are solely those of the author and do not necessarily reflect the views of the publisher, and the publisher hereby disclaims any responsibility for them.

Any people depicted in stock imagery provided by Thinkstock are models, and such images are being used for illustrative purposes only. Certain stock imagery © Thinkstock.

ISBN: 978-1-4917-8288-0 (sc)
ISBN: 978-1-4917-8289-7 (e)

Library of Congress Control Number: 2015918476

Print information available on the last page.

iUniverse rev. date: 11/10/2015

ABOUT THE BOOK

Jenna Aitch, In the High water of Hell, is about an unbreakable bond between two sisters, Jenna and her little sister Doodlebug. A bond which had formed as they grew up as children and grew so much stronger after the loss of their parents quite a few years ago. A bond that runs deep between the two, while to the other they are known as, 'twins of two friends', even though they looked nothing alike besides what's within side. With a strong bond between the two sisters, eyes of revenge soon sets in after the thought kicks in as to when Doodlebug seeks for payback of a foe who publicly humiliated her and her sister. While with the help of a new friend she and her sister had recently made, a man named Podgy, they go out to do just that without Jenna knowing. With the target being the Book of Hearts which Makenzie Drells uses for her girl club, "The Thirteen Hearts", it's not too long after they have it in their possession till it becomes in Jenna's.

Soon after Jenna has possession of the Book of Hearts, she comes to finding out she's one of two who can read from it by the book's creator, Sal'Amanda, the devil's daughter. Just as she comes to finding out that the other one who can is none other than her identical twin sister, Gina, a sister she never knew she had. With the meeting of the book's creator, unveiling family secretes and getting some to start to unravel, she also tells Jenna all about the Book of Hearts plus a whole lot more. While after finding out she was one of two who could read from it, she finds out she was one of two who can save these thirteen princesses told about within the Book of Hearts who lost their souls by trickery by a passing stranger.

Shortly after Jenna reads a story from the Book of Hearts and does like she was told to do by Sal'Amanda, she soon finds herself hovering high above Foot County on a cloud with her little sister, Podgy and another new friend, Breanna. The cloud in-which the Kingdom of Sole that she read about in the Book of Hearts sits on. While with only a few buildings standing along with the castle, to the castle is where they head off to in search for the crown of clouds and the diamond heart shape gem of Princess Antoinette, the key factors to saving her. With a load of traps to contend with throughout the castle, shortly after the crown of clouds and the heart shaped diamond gem are found they're faced with quite a few anguipedes that they have to battle before getting back home.

While the story is an adventurous one from beginning to end, it also holds a little humor throughout the pages within. Just as it's a rewrite of 5ive Aitch, In the Meeting of Manikin Ann. And just like 5ive Aitch, In the Meeting of Manikin Ann, all of the characters in Jenna Aitch, In the High water of Hell, are all fictional just like the story. While in addition to the story, at the chapter's number and title there will be a maze to my heart, heart maze. I've been working on the second book which is called, "Jenna Aitch, In Good to be Evil"

CONTENTS

CHAPTER ONE

Start

THE AITCH SISTERS

Of a town larger than the smallest one known and smaller than the largest known one, lies a town named FallenForHer which centers its self right in the middle of them all. Octagon shape and quite a lively place, the town of FallenForHer is just that plus a whole lot more. While with its three surrounding suburbs Fallen, Her and Dé Blur sitting in a world of their own, there's no doubt that the town of FallenForHer is the heart and soul of Foot County. With the day being the twenty-ninth and the month being September, it sure was a beautiful starry moonlit night that was hovering over Foot County. Cool but not a bone chiller could one possibly call it, well at least not for the Aitch sisters who were right out there busy fishing in the depths of it.

From Hair Curl which is a strip of land that runs from the bank and curls a fourth of the way out in FallenForHer River like a curl of hair, Jenna and her little sister Doodlebug were fishing the calm water of the lower side. While trying out the fishing gear that she received for her birthday from her little sister earlier that day, Jenna knew where they were at was the perfect place for her to do so. With a Midnight Crawler reel attached to a Wormhole fishing pole, the complete setup including the six lures that she also received literally was one of a kind and one which would boggle one's own mind.

Being made for night fishing only, the reel took a special type of string, a spool of flexible florescent orangish-red laser string which resembled the color of a night crawler. Just as the string was merely a beam of laser, it was also flexible like ordinary fishing string. With unique string came glass lens eyes of the Wormhole fishing pole. Having glass lens eyes, it let the string of laser to flow freely up and out of the end of the pole like a regular stringed fishing pole. While being a closed face reel and dome coned, it was painted up to look like a worm hole in a grassy yard. Just as it was battery operated, it had a on and off switch which filled or unfilled the spool of the reel.

Having unbreakable string, it was also un-cut-able too. When turned on the string would automatically feed itself up through the eyes of the pole and then attach itself to one of the six lures that came with it. While each of the lures had a special censer that let the string attach, each of the lures couldn't be separated from the string's connection that was not until the reel was turned off; batteries went dead or if there was too much light around like the light of day. With three top water lures and three submerging lures, the concept of them, the reel and pole were true enough to be unreal.

Being a prize that her little sister won a few days ago from a tagged thirty two inch hellbender she caught while fishing alone at Cane Pole Pond, Jenna was absolutely clueless about how her little sister kept quiet about that for so long like she did. With her little sister's grand catch making the front page of the FallenForHer Newspaper that very morning, that was how she got surprised with the extraordinary gift which she received for her birthday. While Doodlebug's picture with her prized catch that was taken at the park's office at Cane Pole Pond and the picture taken of her with Barb Boon the town mayor there in front of the courthouse while being presented with the prize taking up three fourths of the front page, the rest of the page captured the story.

For as the story went.

~

"A Surprise Catch for a lucky Fisherwoman"

"A local fisherwoman, "Doodlebug", who was out and about fishing around Cane Pole Pond, happened to hook up with a catch of a life time. While fishing there alone and for the first time in seven years luck was on her side when she pulled in this thirty two inch tagged hellbender which gave her an unforgettable fight. A thirty two inch tagged hellbender which landed her a prize worth $5,000.00. A laser stringed Midnight Crawler fishing reel with a Wormhole fishing pole, along with six lures specially made for it."

(Doodlebug) "I never thought I'd ever go fishing again, not after giving it up seven years ago when I lost my mom from cancer and then my dad from heart failure two weeks later. But having empty pockets and being faced with an upcoming birthday which is my sister's, I knew a little fishing might make me feel a little better. While after rounding up a jar of grubs, worms and lizards, it didn't take long to scrounge up a usable stick, a few nuts and bolts for sinkers, some string and a few rust old hooks. With Cane Pole Pond being the only place I could go since I didn't have any fishing license, it was the perfect place to go to be alone, just as that was where I headed off to. While the walk was great, it was late morning when I made it there. Once I found me a spot, I hooked up a grub and tossed my line out and sat down. Just as ten minutes passed by, I felt a nibble, then a small tug and then one heck of a tug. Just as I pulled back, my pole snapped in two and red ants lit up the snapped end of the pole I was still holding like a torch. While the other end of the pole was quickly heading for the water, I tossed the red ant torch aside, got up and went after it. With red ants falling out of it as it was heading for the water, I knew if I manage to get it I would be in for two battles, one with whatever I had hooked and one with the red ants. While being lucky enough to grab it just as it hit the water, I was very lucky to find only a few red ants were left. With very little red ants to have to contend with, it sure was a good thing because what I was hooked up with I knew wasn't a bluegill but a monster and a half. Just as the battle lasted for a staggering twenty minutes, the moment I got my catch into shore I bout freaked out. Seeing nearly a three foot lizard there right in front of me, I came close to tossing the pole into the water and hightailing it the other way. Being fortunate that I didn't, on the count of seeing an orange tag sticking up from the right shoulder, I was fortunate to find out that my frightening catch won me a prize. A prize in-which I can give to my sister for her upcoming birthday. "Happy Birthday sis, I sure hope you like the birthday gift I won for you, I know it's not passes to fish at Lake of the Ocean like you had always wanted to do but I do believe it's a whole lot better."

~

Foot County is a mecca for the fishing enthusiast, a true fishing paradise for all who enjoys the sport. From FallenForHer River where you can catch about anything that swims, just as it separates Her from Dé Blur; FallenForHer from Dé Blur and Dé Blur from Fallen, to Her Lake which sits in the suburb of Her. Just as it's also a hot fishing destination, Her Lake was created when Her Dam was built on the FallenForHer River. Just as there's an ancient lake in the suburb of Dé Blur, Lake of the Ocean which holds quite a few salty creatures. For as Lake of the Ocean is a place where you have to buy a raffle ticket in order to try to win an opportunity to fish it. And there's Starfish Creek there in FallenForHer, another hot spot especially during the sockeye salmon run. While there are several other fishing holes around and about the only place that's not fished a whole lot is none other than Cane Pole Pond.

Cane Pole Pond is a public place to fish and it's a place where you can fish without fishing licenses. But for most it has too many down falls. One of the top three being that it is too small to hold a large number of fish. Just as another reason is, most people became too modernized and don't care for messing around with a ratty old cane pole to fish with in a tiny pond when there were other places they could go. While for as the main reason goes, the majority of people are wary about fishing there on the count of an old folk tale which tells about it being where the severed head of medusa was tossed into which cursed the pond there afterwards. For as it's nothing to see a handful of snakes at any given time string two and three feet straight up out of the water from the pond's middle or anywhere around while shimmering like a weed. Just as Cane Pole Pond sits there in Sole-less Shoe Park which sits right in the center of FallenForHer, Doodlebug's luck paid off when she took the chance and fish there that day.

Knowing that she needed to catch something for her little sister's sake, Jenna knew deep down she needed to catch something for her own sake as well. While having tried five of the six lures within a two hour period of time without having a bite, Jenna thought that it was time to give the last one a whirl. With it being a whoopee-frog which was a top water lure, the green black circled yellow spotted frog was merely a frog shaped whoopee cushion. Just as it had a double bard hook that ran up behind the back legs and pointed out along the frog's side.

Turning off her reel so she could put the instigator away which was double bladed silver and black spinner, Jenna asked her little sister if she wanted to go ahead and inflate the whoopee- frog for her. With a yes being heard it wasn't long afterwards till silliness became the word. Once Doodlebug had the whoopee-frog in hand, she jokily told her sister that she heard if you kiss a frog on the lips it would turn into a prince but never heard what happens when you kiss a frog's hind end. After hearing that from her little sister, Jenna told her that it'll more likely turn into a farting machine just like everybody in Foot County have been turning into. Just as there was a twenty-four hour farting epidemic going around which was very contagious and had plagued the entire Foot County causing people to fart over and over.

With the inflating spout being in between the hooks and rear legs, Doodlebug told her sister, "I guess we're going to find out, that is unless I wind up hooking myself." While placing her lips on the spout, Doodlebug blew a puff of air through it just as it bloated right up. With her wonder wondering wild, Doodlebug just couldn't resist seeing what it sounded like when a fish clamps their jaws down on it. Giving the whoopee-frog a squeeze, the whoopee-frog ripped off a loud squeaky fart. With laughter erupting from her, Doodlebug told her sister that she probably is right about it going to turn into a farting machine because it sure let a doozy of one off.

Jenna is an outgoing young lady who isn't afraid to go after what she wants in life, whether win or lose as long as she tries and gives her very best she always knows that she never goes wrong. Just as she has a certain je ne sais quoi, it is what makes her rara avis amongst all others including her little sister who actually is quite a rare individual to encounter. While being only four years old, older than her little sister Doodlebug who is twenty one; Jenna stands six inches shorter than her little sister for as she stands only four foot nine. With a face of a divided angel, one divided between Heaven and Hell, the combination of the two was the makings of one hell of a gorgeous girl. While having a patch of freckles on both sides of her nose right along with two K cheeks that buffles so beautifully out, both of the two brings out her gorgeous smile that she loves to show to all and to the world. With eyes of emerald green and always sparkling, her eyes are true heart catchers and breakers for as they have the ability to make or break any guy's spirit or mischief will. Just as Jenna also has long soft black hair which runs little ways down past her shoulders which she most generally keeps pulled back tight and tied, she never been seen with her hair curled.

While being short among most all other girls, Jenna isn't short about being athletically built or short about having athletic skills. With the four years of field hockey she played in high school for the, East High Orange Bills, as a forward left wing, Jenna was one of the top five players in the state. Being a gifted player who wore number nine with honor, her dreams of taking her skills to the next level as a college star and then beyond was too far out of her reach. With her field hockey dreams being bleak, Jenna never let the once hungered dream that was too far for her reach get her down for as she knew firsthand what real life was all about.

From being brought up in the poorest part of town there in FallenForHer, which was none other than Grimm Street, the status of how she was brought up from what little her parents were able to provide for her formed her as she grew. For as she grew up to be a wise and a very respectful intelligent young lady, even after the tragic loss of her parents. Just as her mother Jill Aitch passed away from a winless battle of cancer days after she graduated from high school. Her father Joseph Aitch passed away two weeks later right before her and her little sister's eyes there in a Bullpen ring. For as he was a wrestler for FallenForHer's Bullpen Wrestling organization, just as he went by the name, "The Masked Piñata." Just as he was getting ready for his first title match which was going to be held in a steal cage and against Thule Greenland's Giant, Topper, his heart gave up on him from the loss of his wife just as he collapsed in the ring.

Doodlebug, Jenna's younger sister is a curious type of a girl, one who can easily find herself head deep in trouble in the matter of seconds rather than minutes simply by letting her curiosity take control of her and letting it run wild. While being Jenna's younger sister who is able to take the good and the bad without letting herself become troubled, unlike her, Doodlebug is the opposite for as she is more like an out of control seesaw, one who has trouble balancing unwelcome problems out appropriately.

With a face like a porcelain angel that's so fragile, Doodlebug's face holds such a peaceful look as to where one could easily be fooled into believing hope is abundantly full and not a trace of sorrow can be found. Just as she has a few freckles scattered here and there, most being on her high cheeks which brings out her trademark periwinkle dimples whenever she smiles. With bluish-green eyes like dioptase a color shade that differ from her sister's, they have just as many sparkles always sparkling about. While having luscious long pumpernickel color hair, Doodlebug also has a voice that is quite unique and is unlike her sister's and either of her parents for as it's so crisp and clean and so softly smooth like polished marble.

While being an average size girl in height five foot three, there really isn't anything average about her when it comes to her left leg. Being born with only half of leg about three inches below her knee, Doodlebug who's parents didn't have the money to get her a prosthetic lower leg made, took on the task of making her one the day she stopped crawling and started climbing up along the sides of things so she could stand. With many different crazy configurations and off the wall styles from when she was thirteen months old till three years old, one finally stuck with her at the age of three and a half years old. For as she was equipped with an upper leg brace which was securely attached to a pair of straight forks of a kids bicycle with a four inch wheel. Just as like herself, her upper leg brace, bicycle fork and wheel grew right along her.

Putting her at an advantage amongst others with her wheel on the count of how fast she was able to move, it also put her at a disadvantage during her first year of high school as to where she got made fun of and teased allot. While being fortunate enough to make the East High Orange Bills team during tryouts of her sophomore year as number thirteen and as a sweeper, Doodlebug soon became discourage about making the team. For as she found herself having to sit on the sideline week after week while having to watch as everybody else get to play which included her sister just as it was her senior year and the Orange Bills top player. While knowing the reason why she became a bench warmer week after week she never accepted the blame, for as she always blamed the coach for not liking her. While gaining a nickname,

"Hell on a Wheel", it was on the count she never played by the rules of the game. Not only would she trip others to steal the ball but she played barbarically while playing the entire field. While dropping out after the season Doodlebug told her parents she wasn't fooling with it ever again just as she returned her uniform and her field hockey stick.

From the poverty stricken neighborhood she grew up in which was there in Grimm Street just like her sister, Doodlebug was brought up to have good manners and to have respect for others no matter what they thought or said about her. While growing up there in Grimm Street, Doodlebug became quite an artist just as she loved painting just as much as she loved fishing. From her first finger paint set which started it all, to all other types and kind which followed, Doodlebug enjoyed herself with her work. That was up until the loss of her parents as to when she lost interest in everything she enjoyed doing. While the day she decided to pick up fishing again, it landed her on the front page of FallenForHer's newspaper with a prize catch.

CHAPTER TWO

Start

MR. CALAMITY MEET
MISS INSANITY

Once Doodlebug inflated the whoopee-frog again, she held it out just as Jenna turned her reel on and let the string's end attach to it. With a chuckle Doodlebug bounced it out of her hand and told her sister, "It's gassed up and hopping mad." While dangling down from the end of her pole, Jenna swung her pole back and then casted the whoopee-frog out. Just as the laser string went crawling through the darkness of the night trailing behind the whoopee-frog, the sight of the string crawling through the darkness was simply phenomenal. Once the string's end started heading down it wasn't long until a splash was heard. Right after the whoopee-frog hit the water's top so did the string, just as the slack barreled back to the pole's end. Once the string laid lazy on the water's top Jenna and Doodlebug watched as small fishes took nippling hits at it.

With a crank of the reel's handle and a jerk, the string whipped up off of the water just as the sound of the whoopee-frog skidding across was heard. Once the whoopee-frog stopped and the string came back down onto the water's top, Jenna cranked the handle again and gave another jerk. After a few more cranks and jerks, Jenna and her little sister's hearts bout exploded the moment when the water eight yards out in front of them done so. Just as the water's top shattered, Ka-boosh", it got thrown a mile high up in the air and everywhere around. With a huge silvery flash in the center of the mix being seen, hysterical gibberish from both of the sister's mouths became heard but not understood.

Just as the shattered water started to rain down it wasn't too long until the fish came down, "Ka-boosh." With a faintly farting sound being heard the moment that the fish hit the water after coming back down, Doodlebug who was hopping up and down while shaking her sister with one hand and pointing out towards the splash loudly asked, "Did you hear that sis, did you hear that." Before Jenna had a chance to reply to her little sister, the end of her pole drew down causing the entire thing to bend in the form of a 'C.' For as the fish sunk deep and was swimming away from her.

Having great strength to it as it was swimming away from her, the moment it realized that it was hooked Jenna wasn't sure she could handle the fight that it was about to bring. Just as it started thrashing its head back and forth while pulling forward, excruciating pain quickly came to both of her wrist. With a feeling of her hands trying to be jerked off of the ends of her arms, the feel that she was feeling was absolutely unpleasant. While keeping pressure on it and hoping that it would wear its self out soon, that was all Jenna was able to do for as the fish had it where it was impossible for her to turn the handle of the reel.

While Doodlebug was cheering her sister on she forgot about the pole she had out, that was until a ker-splash was heard down where she had hers propped up at. Just as she whipped out her flashlight from her jack pocket, she flashed it down towards where she heard the sound. After seeing her pole was missing from the stick she had it propped up with, she took off like a bolt of lightning down that way. Once she made it to where she had her pole setup at she seen it lying in the water a foot out from shore. While bending over a picking it up, Doodlebug came to find out that she didn't have any fish hooked but she was hooked up with a snag. With her reel being full of water, every time she would push the button to release string to try to get her string un-snagged water would squirt out of the hole.

Being a Hornets-nest fishing reel, the closed face reel looked allot like her sister's Midnight-crawler. While looking like a hornet's nest from the dome coned shape to how it was painted, Doodlebug's reel took nothing more than regular fishing string which sat on a Tree Limb pole. With the pole being a normal fishing pole painted to look like a tree limb, there wasn't anything normal about the sound which the reel would make when reeling in the string. For as it would make the sound of hornets when reeling. The faster you would reel the more buzzing sounds it would make like a disturbed hornet's nest, while the slower you reeled it the less buzzing sounds it made. Just as it was a gift she received on her fourteen birthday and was the last birthday gift she received from her parents before they passed away.

Just as she fought with trying to get herself un-snagged, her sister continued fighting with the fish she was hooked up with. While pulling straight back with her fishing pole and then pushing the release button to let string out, she would reel the slack back in all in hopes of break free from the snag. With it being snagged like it was, Doodlebug had a hunch that she was going to have to cut the string. Just as she laid her pole down on the ground and was on the verge of heading to their tackle box to get something to cut the string, she heard her sister yell, "I got it coming in Bug, I got it coming in."

After hearing her sister yell, Doodlebug was quick about being ready to aid her sister with landing the fish she had hooked. While rushing up to where her sister was at, it didn't take her long to make it there. With the water's top exploding as the hooked fish started jumping as it was coming in, nervous hands set in as Jenna kept reeling in the slack that it was giving. Just as the fish was coming closer and closer while jumping and thrashing its head about, Doodlebug told her sister that she would get ready and grab it and haul it out for her.

Doing like she said she was going to do, Doodlebug got to the water's edge and squatted down so she'd be ready grab a hold of it. Keeping her eyes on the fish as her sister was reeling it in, she and her sister took a drenching when the fish lunched its self out of the water and came crashing down eight feet out in front of them. With laughter being heard from the sisters, it wasn't long after they got drenched until Jenna had the fish heading her little sister's way.

The moment Jenna's fish was right in front of her little sister, her little sister looked up at her with a smile and told her, "Congratulations sis, it's a muskie." Just as she turned her attention back to her sister's catch and retched down and grabbed it behind the gills. While soon thereafter she stood up with it as it was squirming around and carried it a short ways from the water so her sister could get it unhooked and take a little time to look at it.

Once Doodlebug came to a stop, Jenna turned her reel off, laid her pole down and got busy with removing the whoopee-frog beneath the light of the moon. With Jenna's catch not being a monster it wasn't a minnow either, once she removed the whoopee-frog she took a rough measurement of it with herself. While having her little sister to hold it long ways beside of her with the tail's end touching the ground, the tip of the muskie's nose came up a little passed her elbow.

Knowing that it had to be at least three feet long, Jenna took her catch from her little sister and took it back to the water to release it. Being pleased with her first catch, Jenna told her little sister to go ahead and inflate the whoopee-frog and go try to catch her one while she releases her fish. With music to Doodlebug's ears, Doodlebug happily told her sister, "Thought you'd never ask." Just as she picked up the whoopee-frog and pole from the ground and got busy.

Taking her time as she lowered her catch back into the water, Jenna took the time once she had it in to get it revived so it could swim off. Once her catch swam off and she rinsed off her hands and dried them on her pants, she asked her little sister who was on the verge on making a cast where her fishing pole was at. After her little sister told her where she could find it and about it being snagged, Jenna made her way down to where it was suppose to be laying at.

While the night was growing old just as early morning was right around the bend, for the sisters it felt like the night was still young. For as they hadn't come around to realizing that quite some time had disappeared. Once Jenna spotted her little sister's fishing pole she picked it up and got busy with trying to get it un-snagged. Doing like her little sister was doing while trying to get it un-snagged, it wasn't but a minute later until a small burst from the water was heard right along with whizzing sound heading straight for her.

Just as the whizzing sound flew right by her, it wasn't long afterwards until a loud caterwaul was heard, a loud, "Yowl." From behind and from a male who let out the loud yowl, Jenna was struck dumb just as she slowly turned around. While hearing her little sister ask the stupidest questing of, "What was that sound sis, did it come un-snagged and come back and hit you", she didn't fool with replying back. Pulling out her flashlight from her jacket pocket, Jenna flashed it up towards where she heard the loud yowl.

The moment that the light of her flashlight came in contact where she heard the loud yowl, low and behold she spotted a shabby looking middle aged man from whom it came from. A shabby looking middle age man who had the looks which a minority of the high and mighty minded would classify him as being crime's criminal. Just as she looked on she watched as the man was trying to pull a wormed hook out of the palm of his hand. A wormed hook which had a string tied to it that led straight down to her little sister's fishing pole she was holding, just as she didn't know what to think or do.

Standing there in a daze looking towards the man who was working with the hook in his hand, Jenna became quite startled the moment her little sister came up from behind and asked, "Who's that goof, sis." Just as goose bumps ran up her arms while a cold chill ran down her spine, Jenna left the ground about a foot before turning around. With a shake of the head and straight lips, Jenna's freaked out eyes done all of the speaking that needed to be done at the time to her little sister. As a grin of silliness flickered like a flame on Doodlebug's face, she watched as her sister turned back around and headed up to where the man was as at.

While following behind until she caught up and was walking along side of her sister, Jenna told her what happened. Just as Jenna was reeling in the excess string while heading towards the man as the reel was putting off the sound of a nest of hornets, Doodlebug asked her what was she planning on doing once she made it to him. With the stop of the cranking of the reel and the movement of her feet, Jenna looked at her little sister and told her that she was going to try to help him since the fault of him being hooked was hers. Just as Jenna started to reel in more string just as she started walking again, she heard her little sister ask, "How are you planning on helping him, sis."

As they were coming up on the man, Jenna told her little sister, "Just like this Bug." Just as she was about ready to confront the man with the hooked hand, the man yelled out, "Bees", just as he started swing his hands and arms around. After hearing that and seeing the man's actions, Jenna let out a, "Whoa bees", just as she dropped her little sister's pole and told her to run back to the water. Just as Doodlebug let out a, "Geesh bees", she then yelled as she quickly turned around, "Wait for me sis, wait for me, geesh." Just as she dropped her sister's pole and took off while waving her hands and arms around just like her sister who was a mile ahead of her was doing.

Once the two made it down to the water's edge and turned around they asked the other if they got stung. After letting the other know that they didn't get stung, they looked up towards the man. While seeing that he was no longer swinging his hands and arms around, Jenna looked at her little sister and told her, "It had to been the noise from that darn reel of yours which caused this chaos." With a little laugh, all Doodlebug could say was it could have been.

Wasting no time to head on back, shortly after the sisters picked each other's poles up they confronted the man. While confronting the man with the hooked hand, Jenna told him what happened and was sorry. Just as she asked him if he wanted her to take him to the hospital to get the hook removed free of charge on her behalf. Just as she told him that was the least she could do for him.

Noticing that the hook was hooked in the center of his right hand and bleeding with the worm squiggling around, Jenna also noticed that it curved half way in and deep. After giving the man an offer, Jenna was shocked when he turned it down. While having a slushy slur voice as to where a small portion of his spoken words ran off to the curb and became unheard, he told her not to worry about it, things happens. Just as she became a little bit more shocked when he told her that he would fiddle around with it and get it work out.

Letting out a laugh, Doodlebug told him, "I don't blame you for not wanting to go because the last time I remember going to the hospital I left missing half of my left leg by those butchers", just as she pointed down towards her wheel. While right after she went on and told him that they probably would wack off his hand and do the logic thing which would be to replace it with a pirate hook. With convincing evidence, Doodlebug then rolled around an open thought of him letting her pull the hook out from his hand. Just as she told him about the times she watched her dad pull fishing hooks out that he got hooked with including a few from her and her sister. Singing convincing words to him, before Doodlebug knew it her sister let out a, "No way", just as she told her that she would remove it that was only if he wanted her to.

Saying nothing as he looked at the sisters, the man held out his hand towards Jenna and nodded his head for her to give it a try. While turning his head away from the sisters afterwards and looking towards the ground, he knew it was going to hurt. Just as he stood there with his hand held out he listened as Jenna told him once she gets the string bit in two and picked off the worm from the hook she would get started. Once she bit the string in two and got the worm picked off she gave him a warning that she was ready to start.

Feeling pressure as Jenna pressed down on the hook's eye, the man didn't feel anything else not even when she took a hold of the curve of the hook's end. Knowing pain was coming soon, what the man didn't know was what else was about to. Just as Jenna was on the verge of pulling back on the curve of the hook, the man was asked a question by Doodlebug. A question of, if he was heading up the river to prism. For as prism was this huge rectangular stone wider than five school buses and long than three and a half which laid in the middle of the river. With the way and how the current flowed, a huge gush of water would ramp off of the prism every twenty seconds or so. Just as fish could be seen flying off of it during the process. While with her question came, because if you are I heard behind the prism bars the stripers are true brutes, they'll tear you up. Just as there were these four solid stone pillars twenty yards behind the prism standing somewhat in a line across the river with each having a circumference of midsize car and standing from eighty to a hundred and twenty feet tall. With the prism and its bars being in fast moving water it was a common place to go after huge striped bass.

Before the sisters knew it the man became a little hostel after hearing that from Doodlebug. Just as he jerked his hand back causing the hook to get pulled out, he also turned his head and looked straight at them and told them that he wasn't going to prison. While afterwards he loudly told them, all he done was left from a place that no longer wanted him around and wound up here. While right afterwards he told them that he's been trying to catch him something to eat with some hermit fishing gear that he recently found. Just as he point towards the ground at his right side at a piece of stick about a foot and a half long with a gob of string wrapped around it with a hooked end.

Causing both of the sisters to blush, Doodlebug started fanning her face while asking herself if it was getting hot out here or what. While Doodlebug kept fanning away her sister who was now holding the hook, told the man that there was a misunderstanding just as she went on and explained to him what her little sister was talking about. After the man apologized to the sisters and told them that it was a long squiggle of orangish-red light he seen in the night that led him to them, the sisters told him what he seen and led him to the water's edge to show him.

Once the light show was over, shortly afterwards he told them that he had a confession he needed to make. Just as he told them that it wasn't that he no longer was needed as to why he left but it was because he was chased off by these four greenflies. After hearing that, the sisters couldn't help not to laugh. Just as Jenna asked him, "Four green flies chased you off you say", she then asked him if he'd ever heard of flypaper before. While butting in and getting in on the scene Doodlebug added, "Or any fly spray." After Doodlebug finished, Jenna continued on by asking him if he ever heard of a fly swatter like most people uses. Right after hearing that from her sister just as their laughter was boiling over like a pot of hot water, Doodlebug had to go on and add, or the swat team.

Laughing a little with them as he was doing, the man told them that the green flies that he was talking about weren't insects but were these four green men, Darrin, Andrew, Mickael and Nick. Just as soon as the sisters heard that they started cachinnating harder than ever before. With their laughter bringing uncontrollable tears to their eyes, they had a hard time catching their breaths from coughing. While hearing gibberish from the sisters such as, "I bet you a hundred dollars he's going to say he's from Mars where were all the little green Martians comes from", he thought it would be best to say nothing more about it.

Shortly after the sisters got settled down, Jenna told him all he needed to say was that he was vagrant. After hearing that the man gave her a weird look like, "Huh, what are you talking about." While thereafter Doodlebug told him there's no need to feel bad because they too were once homeless. After figuring out what vagrant meant, the man replied in a delente way and said, "Life can be cruel to us all when it wants to be." Just as Doodlebug told him, "It can't it", just as there was such a glimmer of sadness seen within her eyes.

While seeing that his hand was a bloody mess just as he was getting blood strung all over himself, Jenna asked him if he wanted her to wash his hand off and get it treated and bandaged up. Just as he told her that it would be ok for her to do so, she told him more likely it will cicatrize since it won't be done at the hospital by a doctor. Soon after Doodlebug told him, "If you're wondering that means more likely you'll become sick and die." With a little laugh, Jenna told him that it'll heal and more than likely from a scar.

After the silliness was over Jenna washed off the man's wounded hand. While afterwards, she rounding up enough stuff within their tackle box to treat and bandage it up. Just as she open a small ointment bottle that was to treat scraps and cuts, she dabbed some on her finger tip. With allot already happened, Jenna asked the man what his name was right at the very moment she touched his wound with the tip of her finger that had the ointment on it.

In an agonizing way the man bellowed out, "Podgy Littlewhich", just as he started shaking his hand wildly. While before he knew it, Jenna who became irate slapped him hard across the face. After Jenna slapped him she yelled, "Do us a favor and go back to Mars where you came from and have one of those green flying Martians wash your mouth out with soap, you thoughtless galoot." With red marks streaking across the left side of Podgy's face, he had a scared as well as a shocked look on his face as he stared at the sisters. Just as Jenna told her little sister to start rounding up their things so they could go, Podgy took a chance and asked her, what in the world did he do.

Being straightforward as she was known to be with people, Jenna didn't shy around the night's shadow about it for as she simply told him. For as she told him that she didn't deserve to be called a little witch while she was only trying help him. While finding herself put in an awkward position after Podgy told her Littlewhich was his last name, Jenna was quick to apologize to him. Just as she told him her name, her little sister butted in by letting out, "Eee, he, hee, he", like a witch cackle. While right afterwards she extended her left hand and said, "Mr. Calamity meet Miss. Insanity. Once their disputes were resolved and the sisters gathered up their fishing gear they took Podgy home with them so he could get cleaned up and get something to eat.

CHAPTER THREE

Start

AN APERÇU

With the passing of a week after they first met the sisters had Podgy well fed and dressed. While agreeing to let him stay with them of the morning after they met, the sisters just like Podgy watched as a friendship started to grow. Just as the sisters showed Podgy all around Foot County, they also introduced him to a few of their friends. Like Pete and Baby Doll Stump, a brother and sister who live nothing less than the good life there in Dé Blur, just as Baby Doll isn't a sobriquet it is her real name. Right along with Marrian N'Anna 'O and her kooky Jamaican cousin Cinerin N'Anna 'O, who lives a modus life in an apartment in FallenForHer on Bot Boulevard. While taking him to a wayang kulit and a few other shows on the side, the sisters also treated him to a Bullpen Wrestling event that was going on. With some fishing being done at Starfish Creek where the sockeye salmon were doing their spawning run, Podgy had allot of fun.

From all he got to do and the people he got to meet what topped it all off was the day they took him fishing at Starfish Creek for sockeye salmon. Just as the three waded in and started fishing, down from the woods came these six moose. One was a large bull; one was a small bull and the other four were cows. While coming down from the woods they trotted right on into Starfish Creek and stood there at the mouth of Jitter's Swamp where the end of Starfish Creek spills into. Being taken by how big the moose's were from never seeing one in real life, for Podgy it was rather a treat getting to see them. Just as they were right around thirty-five yards away and minding their own business, the moment Doodlebug hooked up with a salmon and was ready to start reeling it in, up in the air it came. For as the large bull moose lifted its head up and had her salmon in its mouth by the tail, just as it was flipping around like a tongue at her. While all three thought it was funny, Podgy told Doodlebug that he never knew moose ate salmon. Just as she replied by telling him, "Moose don't get big and balky by eating grass alone; they have to eat a lot of salmon too to do so." While shortly after Doodlebug wound up with a tailless salmon.

Just as a new morning to a new week came while Podgy was finishing his breakfast, he asked Doodlebug what he could do to repay her and her sister for all they done for him. While being modus about their kindness towards him, Doodlebug told him nothing, nothing at all. Being the type that doesn't like to take advantage of others or live off of others free hand outs, Podgy ask again and then again until eyes of revenge set in right after a thought kicked in just as she told him there was one thing. With her sister at work and with the day being young, all Doodlebug told him was for him to follow her.

Doing like she asked without any questions being asked, Podgy followed her out of the house, up 76th Orange Street and on down Short Run Road which was a two mile walk that led into the town of FallenForHer. Once they made it to the end of Short Run Road, they looked both ways before crossing 900 Street. Just as soon as they found a chance to cross, they headed straight for, "Mrs. Old Shanty's Shack." For as Mrs. Old Shanty's Shack, was nothing other than an antique shop.

Mrs. Old Shanty's Shack, is a heavily trafficked place for both of the Aitch sisters just like for many others. While being the only antique shop in FallenForHer, it's no wonder. Just as it's ran solely by its owner, Mrs. Shanty who's eighty-eight years old, it has never been run by anybody other. While being a dealer in antiques, Mrs. Shanty is one who knows how to get what she wants for pennies on the dollar. Just as she knows how to make those pennies she spends turn right into big beautiful green back dollars.

While whenever somebody brings something in to sell and if it is something she really wants the first thing she does is slip on her rectangular wire frame glasses which has a skimpier set of lens extending out about an inch in front. While afterwards she'll start looking at the item and then start making a eerie low pitch sound, "Hang, yang, yang, yi", a few times before telling the customer that she can't pay very much for reproductions. Just as she tells them that what they have is being mass produced by those ching chongs over in Hong Kong. For as she then will point out a made in Hong Kong ink mark on the item to them. An ink mark she cleverly whips on after placing a finger of hers on a made in Honk Kong inked stamper which she keeps on a shelf behind the checkout counter. While for the majority of the time her deception pays off but every so often it doesn't.

Being a grocery store of antiques with a verity of anything and everything, the moment Doodlebug and Podgy entered, Doodlebug hollered, "Anything new Mrs. Shanty." While hearing, "Nothing new, but a few old things came in the other day and already sold", from Mrs. Shanty, Doodlebug was already moseying her way up and down each of the seven aisles without taking the time to stop and look at anything. Just as Podgy was following behind, he didn't know what to think of it as he was looking back and forth trying his best to look at everything as he passed by.

While he continued following her, he soon came to a stop the moment she stopped in front of the shop and turn back towards the aisles. Just as she was facing the aisles that she flew through, she brought her arms up out to her sides and let them dropped. While right after she told him, "All and good but all of these goods isn't what sis or I are looking for." After telling him that, Doodlebug who now was standing akimbo took notice at this young lady heading her way from the aisle there in front of her.

Just as the mysterious young lady who looked like she was in her late teens to early twenties walked up to her and asked her if she remember who she was. While being completely clueless Doodlebug apologized for not remembering who she was. After Doodlebug apologized, the lady told her, "Heather Sówhich." Just as the young lady asked, "Missing-link surly you haven't completely forgotten all about, "Miss Sandpaper", now have you." While the young lady held her arms out waiting for a hug, Doodlebug mumbled, "Heather Sówhich, Miss Sandpaper what, Heather Sówhich, Miss Sandpaper WHAT", while right afterwards she moved forward and accepted the hug while giving one back.

Heather Sówhich is a twenty one year old young lady and who was Doodlebug's best friend throughout their high school years. While during that time Heather was overweight and had a bad acne problem. For as her face was a spawning ground for pimples which cratered out into puss erupting volcanoes. Being an easy target like Doodlebug, Heather was nicknamed, "Miss Sandpaper" by those who didn't like her. All on the count of how rough her face looked and simply she wasn't good enough for the nose-high group.

While looking nothing like she did during her high school years, Heather Sówhich looked simply ravishing. Just as her hair went from long curly black, to straight black teased with splotches of gray. It also was cut short in the back just as it grew longer as it came around the side while coming to a sharp point at the side's front. With her acne completely gone, freckles became the scene. Just as her lips were sassier than her hips, her sparkling ice-blue Eskimo eyes were completely full of enthusiasm just as they said go ahead and try to steal a kiss. While with a tremendous amount of weight lose, Heather was ironing board thin.

After they finished hugging they asked the other, "What's new', just as they asked each other the same time. While right afterwards they told the other, "No, no, you first", at the same time. Once they finally got coordinated, Heather went first. Just as she told Doodlebug that she's been away in college for the past two years trying to earn her degree in limnology and volcanology. For as she been at a camp for the past two weeks at Lake Volley Ó in Dé Blur getting on site experience for the two.

Lake Volley Ó was the other lake that sat in the suburb of Dé Blur. But unlike Lake of the Ocean, Lake Volley Ó was fresh water which held razorback suckers. While being an active volcano many years ago, after it died half of the top deteriorated while a deep hole at the base filled with water and somehow became inhabited with fish. With a manmade entrance way cut through the side at the base which leads inside to and around the lake, to get to fish it you have to buy raffle tickets like for the Lake of the Ocean and hope that you win.

Once Heather finished, Doodlebug told her all she and her sister been up to. Just as soon as Doodlebug finished, Heather asked her who that was standing by her. Just as she asked if it was her boy friend. While answering her questions in the order that they came in, Doodlebug told her his name was Podgy and he was just a friend of hers and her sister. While right afterwards she told her all about him, which brought much laughter.

Like their laughter, Doodlebug's and Heather's conversation was over heard by Mrs. Shanty. Just as Mrs. Shanty blurted out that she has flyswatters for sell and untested ray guns in case of a Martian invasion for sell as well. Just as she held up this clear purple tinted plastic handgun and pulled the trigger a couple of times causing sparks to flare out of the end. Just as Mrs. Shanty only made Doodlebug's and Heather's laughter grow. While soon after their laughter ended they told each other bye and went on their way. Just as Doodlebug told Mrs. Shanty, "See you later", she headed for the exit door and left out.

Once they were back on the street, Doodlebug took Podgy clear across town to the opposite side of where they were, to E Street. With the walk through town being a dandy one, they stopped at, "Diddly Dog's Doughnuts and Dung-balls", for a drink and something to eat. With a much needed rest while there at Diddly Dog's, the rest was sweet but cut short. After leaving Diddly Dog's, Doodlebug led the way across the street to Goat Trail Road. Just as Goat Trail Road led out of town and into the suburb of Fallen, it also led to the three families that lived there, the Hairs, Breils and Drells.

The moment they made it across the street and was standing on the brim of Goat Trail Road, Doodlebug told Podgy that ahead of them they had approximately a four mile walk. Spilling the beans afterwards Doodlebug clued Podgy in on where they were heading which was to Makenzie Drells house and for the one thing that would keep him in good with her and her sister, which was none other than the Book of Hearts. Just as they started heading up Goat Trail Road which was an old raggedy gravel paved dirt road, Doodlebug gave Podgy an aperçu on what little Baby Doll Stump told her about the Book of Hearts and what happened when she and her sister tried to join Makenzie's club.

Makenzie came from the wealthiest family in all of Foot County, just as she was born and raised in the suburb of Fallen. While standing five foot five and having long thick wavy luscious pumpernickel color hair, she also has sparking dioptase color eyes. Being a ravishing twenty-five year old young lady with a mellifluous voice, she also has an ornery pterodactyl smile when she's up to no good. While coming from the wealthiest family and having anything and everything she could ever want, she never lowered herself by flaunting around to those who had less about what she had. For as she's a respectful person who has much class about herself.

While playing for the Dé Blur Mimes field hockey team during her high school years as number thirteen and as a forward right wing, not only was she the teams top player but she also was the top player of the state. Just as she took the Mimes to four straight state champions and won, she never let her team lose a single game which got them there. Being one who loved field hockey and having succès fou at it, Makenzie also loved magic for as she became quite a magician while growing up while having great success at it too.

Being the last of the Drells, after the loss of her parents and little brother from a car wreck they were in, Makenzie inherited more than the family's wealth. For as she inherited family secrets right along with the Book of Hearts which she recently found out about. The Book of Hearts which Doodlebug was determined to steal with Podgy's help. The Book of Hearts which she wanted to see if either she or her sister could help the thirteen princesses out.

Having so many run-ins with Makenzie, Doodlebug only told Podgy about the most recent one that happen. Happening less than three months ago, it began at Baby Doll's twenty-first birthday party. While she and her sister were there, Baby Doll told them about her turning in her heart and leaving the Thirteen Hearts for good. The exclusive girls club Makenzie orchestrated many years ago in-which she ran and owned. A girls club which jargonize their spoken language into jargon, so if anybody would try to listen in they wouldn't know what they were talking about, it would be gibberish to their ears. Just as the club use to be adventurous and fun, Baby Doll told them it recently became completely opposite than what it once was.

Being curious as they became, they question Baby Doll about what happened. Just as she told them that it all began one evening at the being of a club meeting. Just Makenzie and the Thirteenth Heart looked like they ran through a briar patch; they brought out this odd looking old book which they called the Book of Hearts. While they passed it around letting all members look at it, the book was without words even for Makenzie. That was except for the Thirteenth Heart, whenever she held the book words bled onto the pages. But only she could see them to read not any of the other Hearts or Makenzie.

The day that the book was introduced; Makenzie told them that book had been in her family for centuries and it was made for the one who could read from it to save the souls of these thirteen princesses. Thirteen princesses whose souls were robbed from them by trickery, but whose souls were later captured to have a chance to be saved and finally get to rest in peace. Just as she told them that the book's cover was the souls of the thirteen princesses, she told them that the words within side that the Thirteenth Heart could read tells the story of each and holds the key to saving them.

After a few club meetings and readings from the book for most it was ostensible. That was up until they were actually ready to try to save the soul of the princess that the Thirteenth Heart read about. While only four was to go on the journey, Makenzie, the Thirteenth Heart, Heart Two Sarah Breils and herself Heart Four, they all were excited to go. While doing like they were suppose to do everything went as clockwork and it was no longer doubtable to any of the Hearts. For as what the Thirteenth Heart read was true and not a bogus made up story Makenzie put her up to telling to get everybody heading out on some wild goose chase. Just as they found a place to break a large pool of water to enter the realm where they needed to go the other Hearts stayed behind while staying on guard in case anybody came wondering around.

With the journey being dangerous, just as they had to fight off pack of bones, living skeletons and a three headed panther they were successful at finding what they had to go after. Once they found the crown and emerald heart shaped gemstone of Princess Athena they headed back and left the realm. Just as they, with the rest of the Hearts returned to Makenzie's home, Makenzie told them two other Hearts would get to go with her and the Thirteenth Heart the next time. While afterwards she took the crown and gem upstairs just as the Thirteenth Heart followed with the Book of Hearts.

Believing that one princess had been saved, it was at the next meeting that all hell broke loose there in the living room of Makenzies. Just as she and the Thirteenth Heart came in with the Book of Hearts the look on their faces should had told everybody that something was wrong. As they came in and was getting ready to sit down on the couch, the Book of Hearts flurried into a huge ball of black fire causing the Thirteenth Heart to throw it down onto the floor. While thereafter from the fire rose this female being.

Just as all of the Hearts became scared and jump up from the couch, the female looked straight at Makenzie and the Thirteenth Heart and said well done. Well done at finding the crown and gem of Princess Athena. While right afterwards she told them that it was time to surrender them over. With a smirk followed by a short laugh Makenzie replied, "No chance in hell", while right after she yelled, "Hearts get her, she's here to try to stop us from saving the princesses." Doing as Makenzie asked all of the Hearts excluding the Thirteenth Heart pumbled the female down to the floor to where she literally burned out.

After the meeting wrapped up and came to an end it wasn't long until another meeting came. Before that meeting started which was going to be held outside on the back deck after dark, Makenzie told them that they were going to stop the cacodemon who wants to stop them from saving the princesses. Just as she had everybody to hide in the dark, she told them if the cacodemon appears they would all rush her and forever put her fire out by getting her into the water of the swimming pool.

Once darkness came and all of the Hearts hid, Makenzie and the Thirteenth Heart came out with the Book of Hearts and came to a stop right in front of the swimming pool. Just as they stood there for a while without making a sound the moment Makenzie and the Thirteenth Heart thought she wasn't going to show up, she did. Like before the book flurried into a huge ball of black fire but unlike before the female didn't came from it. While Makenzie looked over at the Thirteenth Heart, the Thirteenth Heart told her, "I don't like this Kenzie."

Right after the Thirteenth Heart let Makenzie know how she was feeling, through the air they saw two Hearts hovering while heading towards them. Just as the two Hearts were kicking theirs legs while swinging their fist up above their heads, they also were yelling for help. Knowing something had them by the tops of their heads, Makenzie knew who had them just like the Thirteenth Heart knew. Just as the two Hearts were approaching Makenzie and the Thirteenth Heart faster and fast, all of a sudden the two Hearts went flying towards them.

While Makenzie and the Thirteenth Heart moved out of the way the two Hearts made a crash landing there in the swing pool, for as the same fate happen to the other Hearts. Once all of the hidden Hearts were taken out, Makenzie and the Thirteenth Heart became the next target. Just as Makenzie was yelling, "Cacodemon come out and show yourself", while she and the Thirteenth Heart were looking all around, it wasn't long till all hell broke loose. While from above and all around the voice of the female said, "I am what is dark, I am the darkness of night and the darkness of hell", just as laughter from her was heard thereafter. After the female spoke, the darkness took a firm grip on the tops of Makenzie and the Thirteenth Heart heads.

Lifting them up in the air and taking them over the swimming pool to its center, all of the Hearts that were still in saw what was about to happen and scrabbled out as fast as they could. Just as soon as the other Hearts cleared out, the female voice spoke, "By this time tomorrow night the crown and gem of Princess Athena must be surrendered." While right after down through the darkness Makenzie and the Thirteenth Heart fell, just as they landed in the swimming pool shortly afterwards.

Just as Doodlebug told Podgy, Baby Doll told her little after Makenzie and the Thirteenth Heart got out of the pool a bouleversement came knocking on the door. A serious uproar that got all of the Hearts questioning if Makenzie had been honest with them or if she's been keeping something from them about what's been going on. Just as the Thirteenth Heart yelled at Makenzie, "I thought we were going to save the souls of these thirteen princesses, not go and steal their crown and gem and use the book to coach out a dastardly evil beings which the other Hearts don't know anything about and have yet to see."

After hearing that from the Thirteenth Heart, Makenzie loudly reminded her that she knew what they were getting into from the very start. While right after the Thirteenth Heart admitted that she knew, she told her she knew it wasn't supposed to be anything like what they were doing. Just as Makenzie told her that she was ungrateful, the Thirteenth Heart replied, "Yeah, I must have learned to be from you', just as she shoved Makenzie causing her to fall backwards into the swimming pool. Just as Makenzie was giving her a baleful stare while look up towards her, she heard her say, "I was naïve of believing that we were going to help out these thirteen princesses, but no longer am I naiveté big chief Makenzie, I'm out of here, so long, adios." For as the Thirteenth Heart quit the club right then and there and with a congé taking place, an abrupt dismissal from the Thirteen Hearts by the Thirteenth Heart so did one from Baby Doll as well.

While Doodlebug and Podgy passed by the Hairs house and were on their way to passing by the Briels house, Podgy told her what she just told him was little farfetched for him to believe. Without becoming mad, Doodlebug told Podgy if she heard that from anybody else besides Baby Doll she would fill the same way. Just as a car drove by dust from the gravel clouded up and blinded their vision while causing them to cough. While vision and breathing condition caused by the dust was a problem throughout their journey, so was becoming dust covered. While suffering it out they kept moving heading for their destination, just as Doodlebug filled Podgy in on the most recent incident she and her sister had with Makenzie.

Beginning one week after Baby Doll's birthday party, there was an article posted in the FallenForHer Newspaper of, "Looking for two new members to join and complete the girls club of the Thirteen Hearts." Even with a bad past we had with Makenzie which was during field hockey games during high school years quite a few years ago, we thought we would put the past behind us and try to join. After reading the article's entirety and seeing that Makenzie didn't just want anybody but somebody with a rare blood type, we thought for sure we were a sure win on the count of our blood type being rare and different from the others. Just as we done like the article said to do, make a profile of ourselves as to why we should be accepted in and personally deliver it to Makenzie.

After the passing of two weeks from delivering our profiles to Makenzie, we received a letter each from the club. With each telling both of us that we were what the club was looking for, the papers also told us if we were still interested in joining there be one task we would have to conquer and once conquered we would officially be members. Just as we were told if we wanted to take on the task we would have to meet up with the club members in front of the post office in FallenForHer at 1:00am in three days.

After talking it over and agreeing to take on the task, we meet up with the Makenzie and the Hearts there in front of the post office and right on time. Just as the Hearts where decked out in their club getup which made it impossible to tell who was who, only one let her true identity be know by voice and that was none other than the clue leader, Makenzie. For as she told us what our task was going to be before getting started, just as she gave us the opportunity to back out.

With our task being combined as a single one which we had to do together, the task that we accepted seemed like a long shot in the dark. Just as our task was to make it to the end of Knee-Knocker Street and back before morning light, we had to do it in a challenging fashion. Being blindfolded and tied together wrist to wrist, elbow to elbow, waist to waist with our backs to each other. Just as we also had the toe end of a shoe stuffed in our mouths with an egg placed in the open end. While having to make the complete run without either losing their egg from their shoe we were very confident that they could conquered the task.

Once we were ready to start Makenzie told us one of the Hearts would follow along and guide us so we wouldn't run into anyone or anything and to be there to let us know when to turn around and head back so we wouldn't step out into traffic. While afterwards she asked which one wanted to be the starting leader, that was after removing the shoes from our mouths. Just as Jenna said she would be the starting leader and I could be the victory leader of them making it back. After the decision was made, Makenzie placed the shoes back into our mouths; got Jenna heading into the right direction and told her and me that we have approximately five hours before daylight just as she told us whenever we were ready we could begin.

Being unable to talk with one another became the down fall of failing to conquer the task. Just as soon as we started moving, we soon tripped one another up and fell down. With eggs splattering on the sidewalk next to us, all Makenzie had to say was, "Nice try, we'll be seeing you in the Monday's Funnies", just as she and the Hearts laughed before leaving. Becoming irate after what we heard just as we were trying to spit out the shoes from our mouths, we knew we been had but what we didn't realize was how bad. That was not until the Monday newspaper came out.

Seeing pictures of us plastered all over the weird and wacky page, even though our faces were blurred it really didn't help. Just as the pictures that were taken of us were after we were blindfolded with the shoes stuffed in our mouths holding the eggs and just as we started walking and just as we started to fall down and after we fell. With each picture being titled, "A loons night out", "Don't go walking the streets a loon", "Fall-loon for you", "It wasn't a loony night for these two." We had no idea how we were going to go out and face the public. While the first month was rough on us, the horrible incident soon faded away shortly afterwards.

Right after Podgy heard that from Doodlebug, he stopped and all he was able to say was, "Man and here I thought I was having it tough from where I came from." With a little laugh coming from Doodlebug as she stood there looking at him, she told him even though she's triskaidekaphobia especially when it comes to the number thirteen which makes up the Hearts, Makenzie is going to get what she deserves if not more. While afterwards she told him it was time for them to start moving again.

After passing by the Breils house it wasn't very long until they were approaching this road that cut off from the main, just as Doodlebug told Podgy, "It's time to become unseen and sneak in." While making tracks as they quickly got off the road, they headed for the wooded area so they could keep their selves concealed from anybody who may drive by. With Doodlebug leading the way, Podgy followed behind while wondering what in the world did he get his self into.

CHAPTER FOUR

Start

MAKENZIE'S HOUSE

A s noontime arrived just as the sun was shining down from high above, the moment Doodlebug and Podgy came to the wood's edge out in front of Makenzie's house they stayed there for a few minutes and scoped the front and the surrounding out. After seeing no cars in the driveway or anybody anywhere around just as it looked like the lights were all off in the house, a few things stood out to where Doodlebug had to question herself. Like the wondrous smell she was smelling, right along with the smoke that was coming from the barbeque grill on the deck which was decked with streamers, balloons and a Happy Birthday Makenzie banner. While not being sure what to think of it other than it could be dying smoke from an early use which was putting off the smell, Doodlebug went ahead and chanced it and came out of her hiding. Just as she moved quickly across the front lawn to the steps of the deck while Podgy followed right along, it wasn't long until up the steps they went.

Once they made it upon the deck, Doodlebug rushed over to the barbeque grill and opened it. While seeing a load of hotdogs, hamburgers, stakes plus other stuff slow cooking, Doodlebug knew they had very little time if any to try to find the Book of Hearts. With a nervous feeling creeping over her, she took a gutsy chance by going over to the front door to see if it was locked or unlocked. While peeking through one of the thirteen glass hearts which were arranged to from one big heart on the front door, Doodlebug saw no movement what so ever. Just as she slowly started turning the knob of the door which was heart shaped and made of dark antique brass which was redden in color, she soon found out it wasn't locked. While an image came fogging up her mind of her opening up the door and becoming overwhelmed with birthday wishes meant for Makenzie, Doodlebug quickly cleared that from her head and prayed that it wasn't going to come true.

Pushing in on the door just as the door opened without a hinge squeak being heard, Doodlebug causally entered in just as Podgy followed. While becoming wowed by the lavishing living room that they were standing in, both Doodlebug and Podgy bout had a heart attach the moment when the wind pulled the front door shut. With the noise being loud, Doodlebug was sure that they were seconds away from being caught. Having nowhere to hide in the living room the two decided to wait by the door for a minute and see if anybody comes around and if so they would be ready to hightail it out of there.

Standing quietly like stone statues there at the door, both Doodlebug and Podgy marveled at the living room. With glossy red wood floors and a circular four piece black leather couch centering it, there also was this round coffee table sitting in the center of the couch. Just as the living room was completely round, four and a half foot up the wall was painted dull white. While the lower wall castle topped around the room, the upper wall which tooth down and around was one with the domed ceiling. Being constructed of glass as the upper wall and ceiling were, it was what could call an oceanarium sight.

With the passing of a minute and a half and nobody coming around to attend to the nose cause by the door, Doodlebug and Podgy couldn't help their selves by taking a tour around the room just to look at the sea life. With a scene of what it would be like to live beneath the sea, all that went through Doodlebug's and Podgy's minds was amazing. Just as sea horses and sea dragons hung around on coral down and around the wall's teeth like a few small octopuses, other fish such as cuddle fish, box fish, parrot fish and porcupine puffer fish plus a slew of small colorful fish swam freely throughout the aquariums entirety. Being such a gorgeous room marveling time soon came to an end after they made a complete run of the room. Once their tour came to an end and they were standing back where they had started, they made their way straight through the living room for this maroon portière covered doorway which had a torchère at each side topped with two small white candles.

Once they made it to the doorway, Doodlebug pushed the curtain to the side a little and had a peek before going any further. After seeing nobody around, they quickly headed on through. While seeing a set of stairs to their left that led upstairs and a closed door to their right, there also was an open room straight ahead for as that was where they decided to head for first. With the walk being short, it didn't take long until they found their selves in the kitchen. While seeing a birthday cake right off the bat sitting there on the table it brought back the memory of the last one Doodlebug was surprised with by her mom, dad and sister.

Being a disappointing time the moment that it happen, it was the day she turned fourteen. While knowing her family didn't have much but made the best of what they did have it never was a problem for her. Just as she was anxiously waiting to open her gifts, she was first surprised with a birthday cake that her mom and sister worked hard on. After coming back home from a morning of fishing with her dad, she was led straight into the kitchen. Just as she was led in she saw this small square chocolate cake with white trimming and with, "Happy Birthday Doodlebug", sitting on the table waiting for her. Being without fourteen candles there was one other thing she saw on her birthday cake. At first glance Doodlebug saw what looked to be like a standing squirrel stand at the end of her name, which she thought was a candle. Right after she joyfully asked where they got the squirrel candle at she soon realized that it was a rat just as it hopped off her cake onto the floor and raced across the floor and into its hole. While her birthday cake was ruin, her birthday wasn't.

Reliving that memory over of her last birthday cake with her mom and dad which had to be tossed into the trash, Doodlebug continued to stare at Makenzie's birthday cake. Seeing such a gorgeous birthday cake only as she had seen in magazines, she looked over at Podgy and told him that the cake is off-limits. Just as she told him, not a figure or even a figure of a thought is to touch it. While there was a bonbonnière sitting on the table too full of candy, there also were a ton of unopened bags of chips piled on the floor beside these two large coolers. Seeing a load of good things to dig into, Doodlebug told Podgy, "A bag of chips, a handful of candy and a pop is ok", just as she grabbed her a sack after opening one of the coolers and taking a can of pop from it.

Taking nothing like she did, all Podgy done was follow her and do as she asked. Just as he followed her out the kitchen's back door and onto the back deck. While after seen that there was nobody around out back, Podgy followed her back into the kitchen and to the stairs and to the closed door right across from them. After being told to check and see if the door was locked, Podgy walked over and checked. Just as it opened right up and a set of steps leading down into the dark was seen, Doodlebug told him to flip the light switch on and go down and see if he can find the Book of Hearts while she checks out the upstairs.

Once Podgy flipped the lights on and started down the cellar after closing the door behind, Doodlebug wasted very little time heading up stairs. Just as soon as she made it up, she looked down towards the long hallway in front of her. After seeing quite a few doors, she looked to her right and saw a large squared opened space. With a large oval opening in one wall to view the fish above the living room, there was a short flight of stairs which led to this balcony above it. Just as she made her way to the stairs and made her way up them it didn't take her long to figure out that it was how Makenzie kept her fish fed and her aquarium cleaned. After coming back down the stairs, she made her way down the hallway.

With family pictures hanging along both sides of the hallway's walls, there also were three doors on each side and one at the hallway's end. While heading for the closest door which was the first door on the right, it wasn't long till Doodlebug opened it only to find out that it was a hall closet. After closing the closet door she made her way across the hallway to the nearest next door. Just as she came upon the door and opened it, she saw a flight of steps leading up to the attic. Doing the logical thing by flipping the attic lights on and heading on up while closing the door behind, Doodlebug done just that.

Becoming ecstatic about how large the attic was the moment she made it up, unlike others which are just a cramp space she was even more ecstatic how neatly and clean Makenzie kept it. With boxes labeled Doodlebug headed straight for this one that said heirlooms of the family. While sitting down her can of pop and bag of chips, she barbarically pulled open the taped box just as old black and white photos from a photo album that was in side of it spilt out everywhere. Being quick about gathering up the old photos and laying to the side, she wasted no time finishing what she started.

Once she had the box open she came across all types of things. While there were two photo albums in the box there were more baby items than anything, such as silver spoons and rattlers with a member of the Drells family engraved on them. With the oldest spoon and rattler having an engraving of 1513, they both were engraved with the name Makenzith Doodail Drells. Just as there wasn't anything that could possibly look like the Book of Hearts, Doodlebug moved onto a different box, a box titled trinkets and odd things. With the same actions being applied to open that box, the moment she got it open she came across all kinds of interesting things.

Being not shy about being a curious girl, Doodlebug wasn't shy about giving this palm size voice changing, voice thrower a whirl which was called the, "Who goes there." While putting it close to her mouth like the instructions said to do, she pointed the other end across the room and gave a wooing sound like a ghost right along with, "I'm going to get you Makenzie." Just as she spoke lightly into the voice thrower, not only did it work but it beefed up her voice louder than what she spoke. With that getting stuffed into her pants pocket, she rummaged on through the box.

After coming up empty handed, Doodlebug looked for a minute or two before coming across this silly looking clown with long arms and legs. Just as it was hanging along side of a wall smiling at her, Doodlebug noticed something odd about its stomach. For as the clown looked like it had swallowed a book. While not being much of a fan of clowns, Doodlebug thought to herself, where else would one hide a book at besides within a clown.

Just as Doodlebug made her way over to the clown and removed it from the wall the clown spoke. While startling her as it said, "You look like Makenzie, you wanna play", Doodlebug became more startled when a crackling sound started to be heard. While the sound was coming from beneath her wheel and foot, the sound grew louder and louder. Without having a chance to move, down through the ceiling she went and with the clowned in her hands. Just as she landed on a bed below which collapsed to the floor, the clown said, "That was fun, now let's do it again Makenzie." After hearing that she felt the stomach of the clown, while finding a zipper on the back she unzipped it. While what looked to be a book stuffed in the clown's stomach was nothing more than a recordable voice box.

Right after tossing the clown to the side and getting off of the battered bed that was kid size, Doodlebug was quick about locating the light switch. After flipping the switch on and quickly realizing whose bedroom she crashed in, a disrespectful feeling caped over her heart and conscience. For as after she flipped on the light she saw that it was Makenzie's little brother's bedroom left the same way before his life was taken away. With stuffed animals scattered here and there and toy cars and trucks, there was this small plastic escritoire with a tablet and a box of crayons on it which caught her eye.

With the desk being similar to one she had when she was little and done her doodling on, she made her way over to it. Once she made it over she read the title on the tablet which was done in blue and red bubbled letters. "The Adventures of Walky and Talky, Two Socks on a Quest to Help those in the need of Help" Just as she turned to the first page, there was a drawing of two socks one outlined in blue with blue stripes and one outlined in red with red stripes, just as both had silly looking faces. While above them it read, "Switched at birth were their names", with Walky written below the blue sock, Talky was written below the red one. Just as Doodlebug turned to the next page it read Walky was the talkative one and Talky was the one who couldn't sit still for very long.

Admiring the artwork right along with the story as she flipped on through the tablet, it brought a few tears to her eyes. Just it brought back some fond memories about an imaginary friend she had and wrote about, "Limby Leen." While the story was short it also was very compelling and unique with a consummation ending. For as Walky and Talky helped Salamander Sam out of an empty sticky jar of, "Granny Jan's Crab Apple Jam", which he became stuck in. Once she wiped away a few tears from her eyes, she headed for the door to leave. Just as she went to turn the door knob, she found out that it was locked so nobody could enter in. After flipping the switch on the door knob to unlock it, she open up the door flipped the switch to relock it and left out from the room. Right after pulling the door to, Doodlebug read this plaque that was on it.

~

"The room of my beloved little brother, Willard Wilson Drells"

"Whose life unfortunately was taken away
from him at the age of five"

"This room is not to be disturbed; he's a sleeping angle now"

"So would you please be considerate and
have a heart, pass by quietly"

~

Soon after reading that, a few more tears Doodlebug had to wipe away from her eyes. Once she wiped away her tears, she turned away from the door and headed across the hallway for the second door on the right. With the one before it on that side being a hall closet, Doodlebug knew that it could very well be a nail in her coffin. Just as soon as she made over to the door, she checked out to see if it was locked or not. With the door knob turning and being unlocked, Doodlebug hunched down as she slowly pushed in on the door.

With the sound of jungle music being heard playing in the room not real loud or not too low, there were two voices in the background which were also heard. Just as there was a male and a female talking to each other, the male being referred to as Burl and the female as Seven. While Doodlebug continued pushing the door open she saw the two at the other end of the room with their backs tuned towards her. With gifts being wrapped up, Doodlebug nearly blew her cover from wanting to laugh so hard when Seven asked him if he heard that ghost any more. For as he heard the ghostly sound Doodlebug made when she was up in the attic and when Seven took a stroll down to check on the food in the barbeque.

Just as Doodlebug was trying to see what Seven and Burl were wrapping up for Makenzie, she soon caught a glimpse of this foot tall charcoal color goofball looking being which looked like a miniature human just as it had a white bushy afro. Just as the being was wearing a miniature pair of blue jeans and a miniature white t-shirt right along with a necklace with a silver peace charm, it was scuffling and shuffling its feet wildly around on the table that they were wrapping the gifts on. Just as it kind of sounded like it was tap dancing with the way its cat-like toenails were clicking as it moved about. While the being was moving around there in front of Seven and Burl on the other side of the gift they were trying to get wrapped, it wait till they had it wrapped before tying into it and unwrapping it.

Just as the being done so while Doodlebug was watching, Doodlebug heard Seven tell it, "Ra-ra Rob, I had it with you", just as she pointed her finger at him and told him, that makes the fifth time he done that. While Ra-ra Rob looked up at Seven with a sinister grin, it jumped up and grabbed a hold of her finger with its hands and started swinging back and forth. While Ra-ra Rob was swinging, Seven told him since he's behaving badly and Makenzie won't have anything to open for her birthday she probably will send him back to hell. After hearing that he let loose of her finger and plopped down Indian style on the table just as he twirled his hands out and let out a mumbling grumble, "rawr, rawr, rawr", as if he were telling her ok wrap it, if you're going to wrap it.

Finding the ability deep down within herself to overcome her erg to wanting to laugh, Doodlebug surprised herself by doing so. While the room was decked out in an African scene, with skins, skulls, tusk and ghoulish looking mask hanging on the walls; the floor was done completely in baboon bones. Having an eerie feeling come over her, Doodlebug figured that it was time to slip away before her hide gets skinned and becomes wrapping paper for a gift for Makenzie. Just as she slipped back and started to pull the door to, there on the floor see saw this brown leather cowboy style hat sitting on top of a matching fringe vest. While being quick about it, she managed to grab both in one swipe with her left hand just as she shut the door afterwards.

Once she got the hat and vest on, she headed straight for the door at the hallway's end while forgetting about the last two doors at the end of each side of the hallway. While knowing she was running on borrowed time, she knew that she was running low on it. Just as the door at the end had a suit of armor from the medieval days standing at each side with a sword and shield, right above the door was the field hockey stick of Makenzie's. Once she made it to the door, no percussion was taken for as she simply grabbed the knob of the door, turned it and rushed right on into the room.

Being extremely lucky that nobody was in the room when she barged right in, Doodlebug was also lucky that nobody seen the door close behind her. For as the moment she pulled the door to, Burl came out of the room him and Seven were in. While as luck would have it, Burl became spook from hearing, "Makenzie, you wanna play", coming from her little brother's room, right along with a flickering glow around the door from the light Doodlebug left on which popped. Just as he wasted very little time at making tracks down the hallway and on downstairs right afterwards.

With her eyes gazing all around it was obvious to Doodlebug that she was in Makenzie's bedroom. While targeting key places where the Book of Hearts might be hidden, Doodlebug targeted the dresser first. Without wasting anytime, the time it took her to search through each of the six drawers of the dresser was less than a minute on the count of only clothes were found. Before she moved on, sitting there on top of the dresser was a couple of pictures. Just as one of those pictures caught her eyes and boggled her mind at the very same time.

Taking the picture and walking with it while heading over towards Makenzie's bed as Doodlebug looked, she saw Makenzie standing at the goalie box there at Orange Bill's field. Just as she saw the unmasked Mime's goalie, Mime number twenty-nine, the one who she had her arm around just as the two of them were smiling. While with the unmasked goalie looking identical to her sister Jenna, from her looks, to her height and everything else besides of the Mimes uniform that she was wearing like the one Makenzie had on, Doodlebug didn't know what to make of it.

As she looked on at the picture she saw much more. With two other individual in the background of the picture with their backs turned and heads slumped down, it was quite obvious who those two were. For as they were none other her and her sister with their Orange Bill uniforms on, helping each other off of the field. Just as it was the very last game she and her sister played for the Orange Bills.

Being conflicted with a wondering thought as she couldn't take her eyes off of the picture, it wasn't long until Doodlebug removed the picture from the frame. Once she had the picture removed she flipped it over and read the writing what was written on the back. "Another year going down the drain for the Orange Bills", "Another year for a state title for the Mimes, no thanks to Mime twenty-nine Gina Aitch and Mime thirteen Makenzie Drells." After reading that she knew her sister had to see the picture and read what was written on the back.

While lay the picture and frame down on the bed, Doodlebug saw this pair of sandals on the bed, a pair which were brand new and with a tag, "Scandaless Sandals." For as the sands were haute couture just like all of the clothes that Makenzie wears. While being in the need of a new shoe just as hers had about seen its better days, she sat down on the bed, removed her shoe and slipped on the right sided sandal. After replacing her shoe with the sandal a thought came across her mind, just as she stood up from the bed, turned around towards it and tossed her hat down on it. Just as the thought was for her to check under the bed and see if the Book of Hearts was under there or not.

After getting on the floor and seeing nothing but darkness, Doodlebug flipped the side of the blanket up onto the bed's top. While getting up afterwards, she made her way around to the other side only to do the same thing with that side. Once she had both sides of the blanket flipped on top of the bed she got down onto her hands and knees and looked underneath. From darkness to a well lighted place beneath Makenzie's bed there beneath it sitting all alone without a speck of dust covering it was this old, 'Heels for a High Society Females', shoebox. While sliding underneath and then like a soldier crawling towards enemy line, Doodlebug made her way to the shoebox. While shortly afterwards with it in her possession, she came crawling out of the other side. With it being the first time she never collided face first with cobwebs or ended up with a dirty bottom side, Doodlebug thanked Makenzie for being a clean freak. Just as she got up from the floor right afterwards and sat the shoebox down on the bed.

Weighing heavily like what was inside of the shoebox that she picked up from the floor, Doodlebug's heart was weighing much heavier. While crossing her fingers Doodlebug told herself three times, "Please be the Book of Hearts", before grabbing a hold of the sides of the shoebox and with her thumbs popping off the lid. With a rolled up motley colored fleece woven from the hair of human which had many tiny awkward looking clear bluish tinted beads throughout it being seen in the shoebox, Doodlebug retched her hands down inside and slowly pulled it up out. While laying it on the bed just as she started to unroll it, she laid her shoe on it and started rolling it up as she continued unrolling it. Just as her shoe was getting rolled up it wasn't long until the end came and a gorgeous hutched back coffer along with an odd looking key was revealed. Just as she picked the coffer up from the bed she took time to look at it.

Being really old and quite detailed, Doodlebug marveled at it as she slowly turned it around while holding it in her hands. With the look of a hunchback chest, instead of it being large and constructive of wood it was much smaller and was made of copper. While being rectangular and with a hunchback lid, the pin which held the two pieces together and allowed it to open were blunt at each end and were in the shape of a heart. Just as the coffer had a built in lock on the opening side which was rather unique and unusual, it was constructive on both parts the lid and the box. With it being in the shape of a heart just as it was carefully dented inwards at a gorgeous curved depth, the keyhole in the center of it had thirteen different size slots. While staring down at the top of the lid, swirling around and going all the way down to the sides of the coffer were these thirteen women who completely covered it. For as each of the women were looking to their left and upwards while having their arms and hands reaching out to the soul that was leaving from their bodies.

Just as Doodlebug flipped the coffer over, there on the bottom she saw a really fine inscription that ran from one end to the other just as she started to read it.

~

'*Beyond the view of each of the princesses' eyes
there was an unknown shadow*'

'*An awaiting time waiting for each of them as
to when their world would crumble*'

'*While within each of the awaiting shadows
there was an evil with such a hunger*'

'*An evil which had a face of a male with the
mind of the devil, a passing stranger*'

'*With three things on the stranger's mind; to
deceive, to destroy and to concur*'

'*The stranger would always picked off the prince
before robbing a princess soul*'

'*While letting their spirits wonder within a
world which theirs had became cold*'

'*The stranger soon met his end after the thirteenth
princess's demise became told*'

'*Without having a true order about his self
besides being anxious to go devour*'

'*Moments after the thirteenth princess's soul
became lost, so did his and forever*'

'*While the ground around him started to crack,
sprucing up sharp peeks of fire*'

'*It wasn't long until this kingdom made of pure
fire rose around him and towered*'

'*With so many devilish faces being seen in the
flames having horrific laughter*'

'*The epic of the firry kingdom didn't faze the
stranger a bit not until he saw her*'

'*The princess whom was without pain and a
prince, the devil's own daughter*'

'*Just as she made her way towards him, the
stranger knew his days were numbered*'

'*With each footstep the princess took, to her the stranger was pulled in closer*'

'*With eyes fix on each others, the stranger cleared
his mind and said not a word*'

'*While without saying a word to the stranger
the princess simply let him burn*'

'*By letting him become human so he could feel
pain as well get what he deserved*'

'*Unlike my father who I hold dear, the stranger
was merely a fiend, a daring devil*'

'*One who was rather clumsy and quite the imp
about the true power he actually held*'

'*While believing he was much larger than his
actual self, a god who was the world*'

'*His arrogance was his admiration just as it blinded
his mind and caused him to fail*'

*'With the stolen souls of the thirteen princesses
being less than doomed which I hold'*

*'They're all being held at a standstill within the
palms of my hands which are immortal'*

*'Just their once wondering spirits are at a rest in-
between but have yet to be internal'*

*'All of the thirteen princesses are waiting for their
final rest and by the help of a mortal'*

~

Once she finished reading the inscription, Doodlebug picked up the key from the bed and quickly looked at it. While being three and a half inch long and made of copper, the key was of the thirteen women which covered the coffer. With their backs to one another and having their arms held outwards while they held each other's hands, the windy swirl look of their dresses from their chest down to their feet which differed from one another was that of the coffer's key. While the key was made up of the thirteen women of the coffer, there was a thirteen bladed heart handle which topped it off right above their heads.

While taking quite a few tries to get the key placed correctly into the thirteen slotted hole, the moment Doodlebug got it in she gave it a turn. Just as the lid of the coffer opened and Doodlebug saw what was inside of it which was a very old looking book, she closed the lid, removed the key and stuck it in her vest pocket and sat the coffer down on the bed.

With so much excitement running through her veins, Doodlebug quickly placed the rolled up fleece back into the shoebox. Just as she put the lid back on it, she picked it up and dropped it down onto the floor and kicked it back under the bed. While putting her hat back on and then grabbing the coffer, Doodlebug rushed out of the bedroom with it under her left arm like a football. With carelessness following her around, not only did she completely forget about the picture that she left lying on the bed but she also forgot to close the bedroom door.

CHAPTER FIVE

Start

LET'S GET OUT OF HERE

After rushing out of Makenzie's bedroom, Doodlebug flew down the hallway. While just as soon as she came upon the stairs and was getting ready to head down them there came the sound of a few females heading towards the kitchen. With female voices she was unable to recognize, Doodlebug peeked around the corner and looked down to see if she could get a clear view of them that was if they walked by. Just as the two females came to a stop there at the doorway behind the curtain there in the living room, there came a thunderous echoing sound which just about caused her to drop the coffer. With the sound being of an electric guitar, Doodlebug had a bad feeling that a big shing ding was on the verge of starting for Makenzie's birthday.

Being lucky that she didn't drop the coffer, Doodlebug was lucky because if she would had it wouldn't had just fell to the floor, it would have taken a tumble down the stairs. Just as the guitar continued on while a bass joined in, Doodlebug listen as the two females headed back through the living room and went out the front door before closing it. With the guitar sounds becoming muffled, Doodlebug slowly started down the stairs.

Once she came to the last step and came down off of it, Doodlebug pulled the curtain to and peeked around the doorway and looked towards the front door of the living room. While turning away and quickly heading for the cellar door, Doodlebug opened it up and hollered down, "Podgy, time to go", just as she closed the door afterwards. After closing the cellar door, she took off through the living room and headed straight for the front door. Just as soon as she made it, she peeked out of the bottom heart of the thirteen heart shaped windows.

With quite a few goofy looking people either jamming on guitars or standing around eating either a hamburger or a hotdog, it didn't take Doodlebug long to figure out they all were females. Just as she kept looking on it wasn't too long until she got a glimpse of some writing on the back of a leather jacket that one was wearing. After reading, "Hell's Hooligans", Doodlebug nearly blew her cover. Just as she bit down on her lip and started hopping up and down with excitement on the count, "Hell's Hooligans", was really a hot all girl band that not only did she like but her sister liked as well.

Having five members, Delusional Dorothy, Dizzy Dead Daisy, Medusa, Metamorphous Corry and Xy which makes up the band, Hell's Hooligans was consisted of metal and rap music. Delusional Dorothy being the singer; Dizzy Dead Daisy being the lead bass guitarist; Medusa being the lead electric guitarist; Metamorphous Corry being the drummer and Xy being the keyboard player and a fire spitter, just as she's the backup for vocals and electric guitar.

While being odd and unique, their looks fitted with their band's name appropriately. Delusional Dorothy had her hair dyed dark blue, red and black, just as it was coned out in long and short spikes throughout the bald spots of her shaved head. Just as she also had her face painted with splotches of dark blue, red and black paint. Dizzy Dead Daisy had her long black hair in dreadlocks and beaded, just as she had her face painted black and white like a hypnotic swirl. Medusa had her long dirty blond hair braided and had her head shaved bald around each braid, while at the end of each braid there was a white skull with flickering red eyes. Just as she had her face painted green and trimmed in black. Metamorphous Corry had her afro sculpted to look like several skulls; just as her afro was black she had the skulls dyed white. Just as she had her face painted white like a skull. Xy, who done nothing with her straight long orange hair or to her face simply wore a red leather devil outfit.

While being lucky none of them saw her hopping around from the other side of the door, Doodlebug was lucky she didn't just go wasping right on out and meet them from being excited as she was. Once she calmed down, she split from the door and headed back to the cellar door to find out what the holdup was with Podgy. Just as she made it to the door and opened it, she heard the knob of the front door turn. While doing the only thing she could do, she quickly rushed down the first two steps of the cellar and closed the door behind.

Feeling her heart pound just as she was able to hear it, Doodlebug started to get a funny feeling that she and Podgy were going to be trapped down in the cellar for awhile. While standing there behind the door, she listened as three of Hells Hooligans walked by and went into the kitchen. With a conversation going on with the three there in the kitchen, Doodlebug was able to hear it. "Makenzie will be here within the next hour along with the Hearts", was what one of Hells Hooligans told the two others. "Yeah and I hope she enjoys the show we'll be putting on for her Daisy, because if we lose our biggest supporter we will be nothing but hooligans", was a reply from one of the other two Hell's Hooligans.

Just as their conversation came to an end, out from the kitchen they came and as they were about to pass by the cellar door they stopped. "Wonder if Makenzie still haves the faceless witch tied up down in the cellar like she did the last time we were here", Daisy asked. With sinister laughs becoming heard and watching as the door knob started to turn, Doodlebug was on the verge of freaking out. While hearing the front door open and one of Hell's Hooligans yell, "Stop goofing around and get out here so we can't practice", Doodlebug watched as the door knob stopped turning.

Hearing, "We best get out there before Medusa blows her top", from one of the other two Hell's Hooligans, shortly after Doodlebug heard three spritzing pops from the opening of three cans of pop. While listening as they made their way through the living room, Doodlebug didn't move a muscle not until she heard them leave out of the front door and the door closed behind them. With the knowledge of when Makenzie and the Hearts were suppose to show up, Doodlebug knew she and Podgy had enough time to get out of there a live.

After hearing the three Hell's Hooligans ranted about a witch Makenzie having tied up down in the cellar all that went through Doodlebug's mind was, "Great, Littlewhich meeting a real witch that couldn't have a pleasant outcome." Just as it didn't take her long to turn around and head on down the cellar steps. While seeing light on at the right at the bottom of the steps as she was making her way down, Doodlebug also saw a six by eight foot book case built inside of the wall which was full of books to the left. Once she made it down and turned towards the right into the light, she quietly called out, "Podg, are you here."

Without a reply being heard, all Doodlebug saw when she entered on in was a rectangular room shelved wall to wall with books. Books that had the look of never being pulled from the selves for a very long time. Just as she asked herself, "Did Podg, run into the witch and hightailed out of here." While wondering if what she asked herself happen while she was heading for the door at the room's end, she started seeing a dim light seeping through right along with a flicker of a shadow. Just as she came up on it and pulled it open, she saw a shadowy figure run a short ways away from her before falling down.

As Doodlebug approached the shadowy figure and saw that it was Podgy, she could tell he was quite scared. Just as his lower jaw swung from side to side while having spooked out eyes, he stuttered a little bit when he asked, "Bugz is that you." While after telling him yes that it was her, he then told her that she bout done him in. After hearing that and seeing the look on his face she apologized, while right after she told him that she found the Book of Hearts.

After hearing that she had already found it, Podgy held out this small heart shaped book that zips up halfway around it and said, "I guess then this isn't the Book of Hearts after all." While taking it from his hand, Doodlebug unzipped it and flipped through the pages. After seeing that it was a diary, she told him that it might not be the Book of Hearts but it sure is a good find, especially for an insomniac like herself when she can't find sleep at night. Just as she stuck the diary into her vest pocket, she then asked if he needed a little help to get up. While holding her right hand down towards him, it didn't take Podgy long to take a hold of it and get pulled up.

Little after he was standing again, Podgy asked her what was with the get up. Just as he was talking about the hat, vest and sandal she was wearing. With an answer of, "Pillage and plunder, that's what we're here for", she went on and told him that she's just like him, half pirate, she has half of a left leg and he had a hook in his hand. While right afterwards she informed him that they had company running around up stairs and they were soon to have more who were a whole lot worse.

Once they made it out of the dim lighted room and the room shelved with books and were facing towards the book case at the bottom of the cellar's steps, an end book on the middle shelf caught Doodlebug's eye. It was a book which read, "Drells history 13AD – 1313AD", on the spine. Just as the book was quite old it also was rather wide too, wide enough to house two or three thousand pages. With her curiosity taking control, Doodlebug made her way to the book to check it out. While placing a hand on top of the book so she could pull it out, she heard a jittery Podgy tell her that it might not be a good idea since they have company and more on the way. With a suspicious tone being heard in Podgy's voice, the moment she pulled back on the book she heard him fly up the cellar steps. Just as she pulled back on the book and Podgy took off, the book case opened inwards like a door while revealing a dreary dark room.

Right after the book case opened, it wasn't but a second afterwards until this Heavenly glow was seen in the far end of the room. While the glow took form it also took control over Doodlebug's emotions. For as the glow took form of what's been weighing heavily on her heart, "Joseph Aitch", her dad. Just as the image started calling for her to come and give him a hug, Doodlebug who was overwhelmed with who she was seeing started moving slowly towards it. Just as she entered into the room while asking, "Dad is that really you", there came a loud shout from a female within the room, "Doodles get out of here."

After the shout, the image of Joseph Aitch caught on fire just as banshee scream became heard. Just as the image caught on fire, the room literally light up like there was no tomorrow. With the walls being shelved with books, they also were shelved with quite a few human skulls for as it looked like a study den for a professor. While the fire raged, seconds after it started it started to swirl around. While taking form of a coiled snake ready to strike, the snake of fire flickered out its tongue a couple of times as it stared at Doodlebug. While before she knew it the snake of fire blasted straight out towards her with its mouth wide open.

While uncoiling as it blasted out towards Doodlebug, the moment its body hit the floor fire gushed out from its sides. Just as the snake uncoiled as it was heading straight for Doodlebug, it wasn't long until a horrific looking being within its coil became relieved. With a hideous looking shag poke bound and strapped to a wooden chair which had long skeletal maggot infested yellowish white hair and long thick yellowish black six inch long finger nails, for Doodlebug it was a scare. Just as her eyes became fixed on the being, she completely forgot about the snake of fire that was heading her way.

Putting great fear in her as the looks of the being was doing, Doodlebug started moving backwards like the words that were coming out of her mouth which turned completely into gibberish. Just as she knew that she defiantly needed to get out of there, she knew that had to be the witch Hell's Hooligans were talking about. With everything happening so fast, another shout from the same female was heard within the room, "Doodles get out of here for cripe sakes." After hearing that shout Doodlebug turned her head towards it as she was moving backwards. Just as she asked, "Rutabaga is that you."

Seconds after asking, out from the darkness came this five foot four, long rainbow colored haired, albino eyed young lady who was wearing a kilt and was decked out for a Scottish festival. While the female was eight feet a head of the fire snake, the moment she made it to the open end of the book case she started pushing it shut while pushing Doodlebug out. Just as the female started pushing the book case and Doodlebug, Doodlebug asked her what in the world is she doing in there. With a reply being, "Doodles, I'm being paid by Makenzie to do a job which no others can do, so please go, get out of here before you get caught, I promises you within three days I'll explain to you everything", Doodlebug got pushed out of the room just as the book case closed.

Moments after Doodlebug got pushed out of the room and the book case closed, from within the room the snake of fire collided with the book case backside. Just as its mouth rolled back, it started rolling its self up as its body kept forcefully moving forwards. While with a doughnut form growing larger and larger as the snake's body continued moving forwards, the moment the tail end came and went the doughnut ring of fire sucked itself in and burned out. Right after the snake of fire was gone, Doodlebug's friend told herself, "Nothing good can come from this", while afterwards she plunged the bottom of her fisted hands up against the wall. While right afterwards she turned around, looked straight at the faceless witch and told her, "And nothing good will ever come from you like Makenzie believes."

Rutabaga, as Doodlebug likes to call her is a very close friend to her and her sister. With Rutabaga, being a nickname for Roorin Tezory, she is an eccentric twenty year old female who dabbles in any and everything of the supernatural and has a masters degree in demonology. Just as she's a friend both of the sisters have always trusted. While having long white hair dyed with the colors of the rainbow, Roorin has eyes that are albino. Like her hair and eyes that are truly white so are the pupils of her eyes which give the illusion of her being blind. With a height of five foot four and an average built, not over weight or not bone skinny but somewhere in between, Roorin feeds off of her studies and work. Just as she dresses to the blood of her heritage; the Scottish of her father which she inherited and the Irish her mother which she inherited. She was told the day she was born there in a, 'but and bens', in Scotland, there was this huge rainbow which was seen that stretched from Scotland over to Ireland.

After seeing what she had seen, Doodlebug knew if anybody could possible explain it, it could only be explained by her old friend Roorin Tezory, "Rutabaga." While heeding her friend's warning, it didn't take her very long to make tracks up the cellar's steps where Podgy was waiting for her at. Moments after making it up, she asked him if he heard anybody pass by the door.

After Podgy told her no, Doodlebug told him to slowly open it and then head for the kitchen. While doing like he was told, Doodlebug followed right behind him. Once they made it safely to the kitchen without being seen, she came to a stop. While seeing a pair of, "maze to my heart sunglasses", sitting on the table out in front of the birthday cake, Doodlebug was quick about snatching them and putting them in her vest pocket. For as they were heart shaped lens which were white as snow with black maze lines. Just as both lens were a maze for an on looked to work through. After sticking them in her vest pocket she looked at Podgy and said, "Pillage and plunder." While right afterwards she let out an, "Arrr."

Once the show was over she told Podgy to follow her no matter what. Just as she took off out of the back door of the kitchen, she cared less about if anybody was back there. Without stopping she continued across the deck and down the deck's steps. While thereafter she headed straight for the wooded area with Podgy following behind.

Just as they started across the yard heading for the woods, there up in the sky behind them a rumbling putting sound was heard. While Doodlebug came to a stop and turned around, she looked up and saw this old doubled winged world war one German relic. With it looking similar to the Red Barron's plane, she knew who it belonged to and who was flying it. For as it was none other than Samantha Buckles, the eight Heart of the Thirteen Hearts.

Samantha Buckles is a twenty three year old young lady with dark brown hair. Just as she stands five foot four and has eyes of the ocean's blue. While being from What County and a self proclaimed flying ace, Samantha rarely is seen without her iron cross sunglasses. Being a hectic person to be around for the most of the time, she is very loyal to Makenzie without a question of a doubt. Just as her favorite saying is ludicrous, especially whenever she's losing a winless argument that she winds up getting caught up in.

While not only did Doodlebug see Samantha flying round in her plane, but she also saw what she was doing. Just as Doodlebug saw, "Happy Birthday", written up in the sky while right below she saw Samantha working on the, "M", for Makenzie. With a birthday wish for Makenzie being already in progress, Doodlebug knew that Makenzie must be very close to home if not at home already. After seeing the plane and the writing, Doodlebug turned back around and took off for the woods.

Once Doodlebug and Podgy made it into the woods they planted their selves up against a tree. Just as they peeked around at the scene of the crime, out from around the right side of the house came Makenzie on a black horse along with Susan Sue Sousashoe the fifth Heart on a brown and white horse. Once they were out in the open here came the others on horseback. Sarah and Aairrha Breils, the second and third Heart; Monique Tüshoe the twelfth Heart, Okie Ka' Bokie the sixth Heart, Regina Sumac the ninth Heart, Amy Poors the tenth Heart and Mirrha Feeart the eleventh Heart.

Being a nerve rattling scene, Doodlebug looked over at Podgy and told him, "Here comes the Calvary of the Red Army." While right after she told him not to move a muscle, not until she gives the word. Just as Makenzie and the Hearts were trotting towards the back of the yard, Doodlebug looked over at Podgy with a terrified look and told him, "This isn't good, this isn't good at all." While staying steadfast there behind the tree as she watched on, Doodlebug heard Podgy say, "Man she looks just like you Bugz." After hearing that Doodlebug looked over at him with a mean look while showing a shaking fist.

As Makenzie and the Hearts made it to the end of the yard, they made their way on across till they were directly out in front of the back door to the kitchen. Just as they were right there in front of Doodlebug and Podgy, Doodlebug thought for sure they had already been seen and were about to become foxes for a hellacious fox hunt. While staying calm and cool, Doodlebug took notice that Makenzie and the other Hearts were marveling at the birthday wish being written up in the sky. Just as they marveled, Doodlebug wanted to laugh so badly on the count of what Makenzie was telling the Hearts.

For as Makenzie was telling them about her first experience of taking a joyride with Samantha a few years ago, a year before the loss of her parents and little brother. Just as she told them that everything was going fine up until the engine started puttering and Samantha let out an uh-oh that's not good. While hearing that they were out of gas and were going to crash, that was when the plane took a nose dive straight down and started spinning around. With so much screaming going on from Samantha as they were going down, Makenzie told them all that came out of hers was her breakfast and lunch. For as she chucked up her breakfast and lunch right along with whatever else was in her intestines and gut as they were going down.

While a stream of gunk was flowing up from the side of her mouth as they were going down, she soon heard laughter from Samantha. Just as they were a few feet from plowing nose first into the ground, the engine kicked on and Samantha pulled back on the throttle and yelled psych. The moment Samantha flipped on the engine and pulled back on the throttle and had the plane heading up, Makenzie told them that she watched as what she chucked up come down. Just as she told them shortly after Samantha landed the plane she chased her around the plane quite a few times and to hell's half acres afterwards to get her hands on her for what she done. Just as she told them Samantha got away from her and that day and the incident soon became forgotten up until now.

With humor being found in Makenzie's story, Susan told her that she sure wouldn't go up there with Samantha. While a few other Hearts said the same thing, Sarah told them that Samantha got her up there once only to come swooping down to barnstorm her barn. With more laughter being heard, Doodlebug heard Makenzie say, "I'll never go back up ever again with her." After a few minutes passed by, Doodlebug was relieved when she heard Makenzie tell the Hearts, "Come on lets go."

After hearing that, Doodlebug watched as they made their way on to the other side of the yard just as she heard Makenzie say, "After the party I'll be heading to Hope County to try to find Gina so I can try to make things right with her." Just as they made their way down afterwards and right by the left side of the house. Once they were out of sight, Doodlebug who was sweating bullets looked over at Podgy and told him that was a close one. While right afterwards she told him that it was time for them to make tracks and fast. Just as she took off as fast as she possibly could go through the thick woods.

With the terrain being woolly, thick and hilly it was also quite rough and rugged in many places. While having many skimpy ankle deep creeks they had to cross right along with some wide knee deep streams which stay fog covered, the Double-Blacks that Doodlebug and Podgy were venturing through were also somewhat dark, dreary and shadowy. Just as the Double-Blacks where made up of ninety-five percent of pine trees and five percent of gum and oak trees with patches of laurel bushes here and there, the ancient forest was also made up with slew of different types of insects and animals. Being a none hunting ground and a place that never been touched by an axe, a blade or a chain of a lumber jacks saw, beside the outer skirt where the Hairs, Breils and Drells lived, the Double-Blacks were rarely treaded on by human.

CHAPTER SIX

Start

NOT TO BE SPEAKING BOMBASTICALLY

While nearly traveling twenty-two miles within the time frame of sixteen hours, the moment Doodlebug and Podgy came out of the Double-Blacks they were truly worn out. From early in the evening when they headed in till late the next morning to when they came out, neither of the two found any sleep throughout the night, for as they constantly stayed on the move. Just as they conquered the highest point in Foot County on their journey, a mammoth size mountain called Halo Hill which has a staggering elevation of six thousand and eight hundred and eighty six feet. For as it is a mountain that can be seen nearly anywhere in the county's region towering high with a cloud made of thick white fog haloing near its top. Just as they came out of the Double-Blacks it wasn't long afterwards until they found out where they ended up at, just as they ended up in, "What County."

With What County being twenty-one and a half miles away from Foot County, the moment Doodlebug called home from a payphone outside of, "Green Boogies Burgers", and told her sister where she and Podgy where at the first thing she heard her sister say was, "WHAT", very loudly. While after getting a scowling over the phone and then on the way home, sleep was deprived from her and Podgy up until they explain their actions for the hundredth time while sitting there at the kitchen table. Just as the two crashed there at the kitchen table afterwards, Jenna took time to look at the coffer.

Being taken with the design and the designs on the coffer, the script on the bottom was absolutely phenomenal. Seeing that it took a key, she had to assume that either her little sister or Podgy had it on them. While wanting to wake them up and see, Jenna figured that it probably be useless to try on the count of their sleep wouldn't let their mind's break free. Knowing that the Book of Hearts was inside of the coffer like her little sister had told her, what Jenna never knew was that there was a coffer to begin with which held the book.

Realizing that there had to be so much more to what she had already learned from the little she had already learned about the Book of Hearts, Jenna had a feeling once her little sister and Podgy woke up she would know a little more if not a whole lot. While being anxious for them to wake up, Jenna sat quietly in the living room on the couch while marveling at the coffer and rereading the script on the bottom over and over. With time going by slow it wasn't long until she zonked out there on the couch.

Little after falling asleep Jenna quickly woke up after a loud ka-thonk sound nearby her was heard. Just as she jumped up and looked around, it didn't take her very long to figure out where the sound came from. After seeing nothing around, she looked straight down and saw the coffer lying on the floor near her feet. While realizing that it must have broken free from her hands when she dozed off and rolled off the couch, she thought not much else of it besides picking it up.

Just as she started to bend over to pick it up, up from around the seam of the coffer fire which was pitch black as the devil's own soul starter to emerge and rapidly grow. While stepping back, Jenna watched as the black fire took form of a sinister looking woman. With long black hair, hair that was strains of the black fire, the woman also had skin that was white as snow. While her eyes were funnels of hell's fire, screams of lost souls could be heard crying out from within her pupils if within them you stared to long. Just as she stood right at six foot tall, the woman wore a black dress which was made from the black fire just like the elbow length gloves she wore.

Being without any jewelry besides a necklace, the necklace which she wore was rather unique just like the amulet that it carried. While the necklace was black as the fire that created her, it didn't have a burning look. For as the necklace that she wore looked merely like a thin piece of string but looked so cold. Just as the amulet that it was attached to was six black claws which held this hexagon shape stone which was an inch by an inch in size. While for as the stone went, around the sides and the side's top it looked like rumbling fire underneath glass while the center of the stone was pitch black. Like her very own eyes the stone was pretty much a fitting match.

After the woman was in full form just as she never took an eye off of Jenna, the woman said, "Gina, Gina, Gina, let me guess, they're all hiding and going to try to jump me from behind again." With a short laugh right after, the woman moved forward so fast and clutched Jenna by the throat and lifted her up off of her feet. While being unable to scream for help all Jenna was able to do was kick at the woman while trying to pry the woman's hands loose from her throat. Just as the woman looked up towards Jenna while having a bitter look on her face, she shook her head and told her, "You're not Gina, you're soul is different from hers."

Having such a ferric tone in her voice that was full of anger, the woman asked Jenna where Gina and Makenzie were hiding along with the rest of their costume wearing crew. After hearing Makenzie's name being mentioned Jenna only could think the worst. While finding herself flying through the air backwards, it wasn't long until she collided with the recliner. Just as it reclined out as it toppled over with her, the crash caused a few pictures hanging on the wall and her Orange Bills high School field hockey stick to jar loose and fall down.

Playing it smart by staying down and hiding behind the recliner's side, Jenna knew if she would get up she would become an easy target. Just as she peeked up from the recliner's side to see if the woman was still there or where she was while clenching onto her field hockey stick, the moment Jenna peeked up she had no choice but to sprout up from her hiding and yelled, "Hey you." After getting the woman's attention just as she stopped and turned around, Jenna knew she had to keep her from going into the kitchen at any means necessary for as that was where her little sister and Podgy were sound asleep at. While Jenna watched as the woman started heading her way, she held out her field hockey stick towards her and dropped a bomb shell which stopped her in her tracks.

With the bomb shell that Jenna dropped being merely a question of, 'Who are you", it was enough to bring peace for the time being and for her and the female to talk. While Jenna came out from around the recliner and into the open, she listened as the woman told her, her name. With Sal' Amanda being the female's name, she also told her that she was the darkness of hell and the daughter of the prince of darkness. After hearing that Jenna told her, her name. Just as the two moved closer, Sal' Amanda told Jenna that she must know the Drells, the one who is called Makenzie or if not in her possession she wouldn't now be in. As Sal' Amanda moved closer just as Jenna stopped, she told her, surly she knew her own sister, her sister who's identity is identical to hers, her identical twin Gina Aitch.

After hearing that from Sal' Amanda, Jenna admitted that she did know Makenzie Drells but they were far from being friends. While thereafter she told Sal' Amanda that she didn't have a twin sister. Just as she went on and told her that she did have a younger sister who was four years younger than her and looked very little like her. Just as Sal' Amanda stopped; Jenna went ahead and told her all about her little sister's recent adventure and the reason why she went on it. With humor being found in the story just as Sal' Amanda laughed a little, it wasn't long after until Jenna heard a click out in front of her on the floor.

Just as she took her eyes off of Sal' Amanda and looked where the sound came from, she saw that it came from the coffer just as she watched as it opened. Right after the coffer opened, out from within side of it came the Book of Hearts. While Jenna watched as the Book of Hearts rose up, she also watched as the lock of hair which sealed it come unfasten. Once the book became unsealed, it came to a stop in midair and opened up to the center just as the lock of hair fell down in the crease like a book marker.

Before Jenna had a chance to say anything, Sal' Amanda beat her to the punch. Just as Sal' Amanda told her if she wanted to find out if she could save the lost souls of the thirteen princesses all she had to do was to look and see if the words of the princesses would bleed on the book's pages for her. Just as Jenna slowly made her way over towards the Book of Hearts, Sal' Amanda told her, if in fact the words do bleed on then that could only mean Gina is your sister. Without saying anything to Sal' Amanda the moment she came upon to the Book of Hearts, she watched as words bled on the pages.

As Jenna started reading silently, her attention soon became focused on Sal' Amanda, just as she took her eyes off from the writing in the book and looked straight at her. While hearing Sal' Amanda's voice speaking to her from within her mind, she told Jenna that she has the ability to save the lost souls of the thirteen princesses, just like Gina her identical twin sister. After hearing Sal' Amanda speak to her that way, Jenna watched as the Book of Hearts close up and become sealed up with the lock of hair. Just as the book dropped, it fell straight down into the coffer just as the lid closed and it became locked.

After the Book of Hearts became locked back inside of the coffer Jenna asked Sal' Amanda what she must do to save the lost souls of the thirteen princesses. With much sincerity being heard from Jenna just like the look on her face, Sal' Amanda just stood there looking at her. While Sal' Amanda was trying to look through Jenna to see if her sincerity was real or not, it wasn't long until she heard Jenna ask her the same question once again. Just as Sal' Amanda took a couple of steps forward she told Jenna, "So sincere was that of your twin sister Gina, so sincere she with Makenzie accomplished the very first step to save the souls of the thirteen princesses."

With a short pause while not taking her eyes off of Jenna, Sal' Amanda slid clapped her hands together. While causing a blaze of orange-ish red fire to swirl out, it grew as it swirled around while heading towards Jenna. Once the swirl of fire came to a stop less than three feet in front of her, she watched as steps of fire form around inside. After the steps became formed, she saw Makenzie and the one called Gina running down the steps of fire plus a whole lot more.

While Makenzie had the coffer in her hands and was leading the way, they were being chased by fiends. The fiends were miniature men like beings with clodhopping heads which stood no larger than a foot and a half tall. Just as they were charcoal colored, they were toothy and had claws like a cat. While there were quite a few casing after them, there were others that were popping out of the firry wall and up through the steps grabbing at them trying to cause them to fall.

Being quite a nuisance like the fiends were just as they didn't desist, they became much more of a nuisance every time Makenzie stopped. While images of bad things she done in the past came to haunt her causing her to stop, it gave an open opportunity for the fiends to attack and try to push her and Gina off of the steps to their doom. Just as Gina had to fight off the fiends while Makenzie had to relive the bad memories, she also had to fight off winged demons that took swats at them. Wing demons which constantly swatted at the wicketest of the wicket, people who were already falling down to the bottomless pit of hell while reliving their wrong doings over and over again. Being without a tainted past there was nothing bad for Gina to have to relive, while she couldn't see the bad memories that Makenzie would frequently have neither could Jenna.

With the scene being horrific, it wasn't long until Makenzie and Gina came to a stop. While being ready for an attack, Makenzie and Gina watched as the fiends either, jumped off the steps, ran back up them or hide within them or within the wall. Having the wonder of why they didn't attack, the answer soon became clear. Just as they turned back around towards the emptiness of pure darkness out in front of them and below them, up from the dark came a burnt blistery red winged male being. Just as he had two horns one at each side of his head with one being half broken, the being also had threads of white hair that coiled back which verily covered his scalp. With jagged rotted teeth and black brittle fingernails the male being had eyes that were yellow. Just as he was shackled at the wrist, the chains from them dangled down to the obis from where he came from. For as it was obvious that the male being was none other than the devil himself.

Just as Jenna watched as the devil came face to face with Makenzie and Gina, she wasn't able to tell who had the most sinister smile between him and Makenzie. While the three stared at each other, the devil was the first to speak. With a voice like a dragon, the devil asked Makenzie and Gina why they were there. Being unintimidating to Makenzie, she told him who she and Gina were and who sent them down there. While right afterwards Makenzie held out the coffer and told him that it was the key which would unlock it that they were after.

Saying nothing else, Makenzie and Gina watched as he fell away, falling outwards towards the center of the emptiness. As the devil came to a stop his head dropped down like his arms and hands. While the two looked on just like Jenna, they watched as the devil curled his hands back and forth motioning for whatever was down below him in the obis to come up. As the devil motioned on it wasn't long until up from the obis came this winged demon which had its claws of its clawed feet sunk deep within the head of this screaming baldheaded human male. Once the demon came to a stop, it held the human male directly out in front of the devil.

Just as Jenna heard Sal' Amanda tell her, that was the stranger, the one who robbed the souls of the thirteen princesses by trickery. While right after she heard her say, "The day he tried to trick her and rob away hers became his down fall for as he found out a soul she didn't have." While Jenna watched on, she listened to what else Sal' Amanda had to say. Just as Sal' Amanda told her that at his down fall the souls of the thirteen princesses she captured from him, while to hell she let him descend not as his true self but as a human.

While the demon held the stranger out in front of the devil the devil just stared at him. With a smile there came a laugh right along with mumbling gibberish that was never before heard. Just as Makenzie and Gina watched while listening to the devil's mumbling gibberish, it wasn't long until crackling sounds became heard. While the stranger started to shrivel and shrink, every bone in his body started to crack. Without any of his bones piercing through his skin as he shrunk, the stranger's bones started to take a new form.

From a fully grown male to a three inch tall skin covered object, the sight was absolutely unreal. Just as the wing demon held on, it wasn't long until from the mouth of the devil spewed a copper mist which covered the shrunken stranger. After the mist took hold, a key was reviled. A thirteen bladed key in the form of the thirteen princesses topped with a thirteen bladed heart handle. Once the key was form the winged demon flew over to the devil and dropped it within the palm of his right hand.

Right after the wing demon dropped the key off to the devil, the devil made his way over to Makenzie and Gina. Once he came upon them and came to a stop, he placed the key in the keyhole of the coffer and turned it. Just as the lid popped open, it only opened enough to let them know that the key worked. Without saying anything, the devil closed the coffer lid, removed the key and handed it to Makenzie.

Just as the devil fell away from Makenzie and Gina, he fell away and down to the obis from where he had came. Once the devil was out of sight, Jenna watched as Makenzie handed the key to Gina before they high tailed it up the firry steps. While Gina led the way up just as both had the fight with the fiends and winged demons once again, Gina had to keep looking back to make sure nothing in Makenzie's past caught up with her to cause her to stop. Just as Jenna watched as they were running up, the moment when they were about to reach the top she seen this fiend that had a clump of white hair like an afro jump and latched onto Makenzie's derrière.

Right after seeing the fiend latch onto Makenzie, Jenna's attention was drawn away. For as her attention was drawn away from a loud curious voice she heard. A loud curious voice which came from the doorway of the kitchen. A loud curious voice which hollered out, "Not to be speaking bombastically but who in hell are you", which came from none other than her little sister, Doodlebug.

CHAPTER SEVEN

Start

WHAT YOU MUST DO

With Doodlebug's question of curiosity pulling her sister's eyes towards her right along with Sal' Amanda's who turned around in her direction, it also caused the swirl of fire to break apart and die out. Before Jenna had a chance to say anything to her little sister, Sal' Amanda already had a mouthful on the way. For as Sal' Amanda told Doodlebug, "If I were delusional and didn't know any better I would say, Makenzie you already know who I am but since I'm not and you're not Makenzie I'll tell you." Just as she told her, "In hell they call me, Sal' Amanda." After Sal' Amanda told Doodlebug who she was, out from the kitchen came this tabby cat. Just as the tabby cat had a small palm size radio harness to its right side while wearing a small derby hat on its head. While music was playing from the radio that it wore, it came to a stop beside Doodlebug. Just as it looked towards Sal' Amanda and stood up on its hind legs like a groundhog and started working its arms up and down out in front of her, Jenna told her little sister to take Boom-box Boob up to her room. Just as Boom-box Boob was both of theirs and was a cat that never learned to purr.

Doing like her sister asked, Doodlebug picked Boom-box Boob up and made her way right by Sal' Amanda and on through the living room. Just as she started up the stairs, Jenna told her not to forget to close the door so she won't follow her right back down. While saying nothing, Doodlebug continued up. Once Doodlebug made it up the stairs, Sal' Amanda told Jenna, "So sincere was that of your twin sister Gina, so sincere she with Makenzie along with two others accomplished retrieving the crown and gem of Princess Athena."

While Jenna replayed in her mind what Baby Doll told her and her little sister three months ago at her birthday party, she heard Sal' Amanda say, "But her sincerity soon came to an end when she failed to convince Makenzie to let her surrender the crown and gem over like they were told they had to do." While remembering what Baby Doll told her and her little sister, Sal' Amanda looked straight at her and told her, "Your thoughts from me you can't hide." After hearing that Jenna let the memory come to an end just as she questioned Sal' Amanda why she don't just take the crown and gem from Makenzie. Without any hesitation Sal' Amanda told her that she couldn't, because

Gina has to be the one who hands them over by placing them on the Book of Hearts. By whom is a descendant of the stranger, as of whose blood matches his and the princess he seduced.

Causing a weird look to come upon Jenna's face after hearing that, she asked Sal' Amanda if she meant that she's a descendant of the stranger and a princess he seduced. As Sal' Amanda stared at her, she told her that was correct and her twin is a descendant as well. After telling Jenna that, Sal' Amanda told her that the wrong he done was up to her or her twin Gina to make things right. Just as she told her only they could surrender the crown and gem over and nobody else.

After Sal' Amanda told Jenna that, Doodlebug was heard as she came trotting down the stairs. While Sal' Amanda not only had a view of Jenna but she also had a view of the stairs behind her. Just as Sal' Amanda watched as Doodlebug was making her way down the stairs while looking towards Jenna, she went on and told Jenna a little bit more about Gina. While telling her not only did her twin fail to convince Makenzie to let her surrender the crown and gem of Princess Athena over but she also helped Makenzie to lure out one of the wicketest beings from the Book of Hearts.

Before Sal' Amanda had a chance to continue on, Doodlebug asked if it was the faceless witch that she was talking about. While right afterwards she told Sal' Amanda that she seen it strapped to a chair in a hidden room down in the cellar of Makenzie's home. Just as she went on and told her what happened the moment she saw her down there. With an answer of yes she's the one coming from Sal' Amanda, Sal' Amanda told Doodlebug that she was very lucky to be alive to tell about it.

Once Doodlebug made in down the stairs, she made her way over to her sister. Just as Sal' Amanda stared at them standing side by side, within her mind she told herself déjà vu. While Sal' Amanda stared, Jenna asked once again what must she do to save the souls of the thirteen princesses. Just as she told Sal' Amanda, she and her little sister are nothing like Makenzie.

With a smile Sal' Amanda told her shortly she would know but before that there are other things she needs to know first. While beginning with the cover of the Book of Hearts being the souls of the thirteen princesses, she moved on to the lock of hair that sealed it. Just as she told Jenna that the lock of hair is made up of thirteen strands of hair from each of the thirteen princesses. And that the lock of hair is like a lock, a lock to prevent anything from straying out whenever the book isn't in use. Just as she told her, every time she's through reading she'll have to seal the book back up with the lock of hair and without breaking a strand of the hair.

Without saying anything just as she and her little sister listened on, Sal' Amanda told Jenna that the lock of hair was the first lock in preventing any lively beings from straying out just like the second lock. Just as she told her that is a fleece, a fleece made of the hair of the thirteen princesses and beaded with the thirteen last drops of tears which they cried. After hearing that Doodlebug told Sal' Amanda she saw the fleece at Makenzie's house. Just as Doodlebug told her that it was stuffed in a shoebox under Makenzie's bed while wrapped around the coffer and the key.

After telling Sal' Amanda that, Doodlebug told her shortly after she found the coffer and the key she rolled the fleece back up, stuffed it back into the shoebox and slid it back under Makenzie's bed. Once Doodlebug finished, Sal' Amanda said that the fleece was a lock which must be wrapped around the book when not in use to prevent spirits evil and none evil from escaping and wondering the world. With a freaked look coming upon Doodlebug's face after hearing that she looked over at her sister and said, "Uh-oh." While not knowing what to think, all Doodlebug knew was that it would be a suicide mission to try to go back for it.

As Sal' Amanda listened to what Doodlebug told her, she replied by telling her that there was also a third lock which protected the book from anything escaping. For as it was none other than the coffer. After telling Jenna about the three locks and what their purpose were, Sal' Amanda went back to the Book of Hearts. Just as she told Jenna within the book there are thirteen stories for each of the princesses.

Thirteen stories only she will be able to see to read, that was beside her twin sister Gina. Just as Doodlebug heard that, she looked over at her sister and asked, "She already told you that you have a twin", while pointing towards Sal' Amanda.

Having a surprised look on her face like the tone that was in her voice as she asked her sister, one came upon Jenna's face and in her voice when she asked her little sister what in the world was she talking about. After Doodlebug explained to her sister about the picture she saw in Makenzie's bed room, she said, "If you don't believe me, here take a look at it for yourself", just as she then retched her left hand in her vest pocked. While feeling around in the pocket for the picture, Doodlebug told her sister to hold on for a second because she knew she had it. Just as the left pocket was picture less but not empty just as the key to the coffer was in it, Doodlebug didn't give it any thought to give it to her sister. After finding no picture in her left pocket she tried the right pocket just as she scrambled her hand around in it only to find emptiness that was besides the heart shaped diary and the maze to my heart sunglasses.

While blurting out, "Great", in frustration, Doodlebug tried thinking back after coming across the picture back in Makenzie's bed room. Just as she remembered taking it out of the frame that it was in, she also remembered laying it down on the bed shortly after becoming distracted by the scandaless sandals. With her mind rolling like a runaway barrel, Doodlebug remembered after changing her shoe for one of the sandals, she looked under Makenzie's bed and came across the shoebox that had the coffer inside of it. While realizing one thing leading to the other, Doodlebug realized she plumb forgot about leaving the picture lying on the bed.

Believing what Sal' Amanda had told her about having a twin sister and what she had showed her had to be a lie, the moment her little sister told her all about the picture she didn't want to believe that it was true just as she really wanted to cry. After Doodlebug remembered leaving the picture on Makenzie's bed she told her misfortunate mishap to her sister. Just as Jenna was holding in the tears she wanted to cry, she told her little sister they would figure everything out in a little while. While right afterwards she looked at Sal' Amanda and asked if her little sister could read from the Book of Hearts.

With their eyes focused on Sal' Amanda, awaiting to hear what she had to say, it wasn't long until they got an ear full. Just as she told Jenna, "No, her little sister wouldn't be able to." While right after she told her that, the Book of Hearts has one keeper the blood line of a true Drells. Just as she told her that the Book of Hearts has one which is of two who has the ability to save the princesses' souls, a true Aitch whose blood line is of the stranger and of a princess who he seduced. And afterwards she told her that there is one judge who has the ability to overpower any spirits or beings which may escape from within the Book of Hearts and send them back.

After telling Jenna that, she told her that the judge has a blood line of a true Drells and of a true Aitch. Just as Sal' Amanda turned her attention away from Jenna and looked straight at Doodlebug. While afterwards she told Doodlebug, in time she would understand and in time she would have to face the faceless witch of hades if not others. With that being said from Sal' Amanda, Doodlebug turned white as a ghost and muttered to herself, "I have Drells blood running through my veins, what, I have Drells blood running through my veins, WHAT." Just as she fainted right afterwards and fell ever so lightly to the floor.

With it happening so fast, Jenna had no time to catch her even though she was stand right beside of her. While rush down to the floor to her little sister's aid, Jenna lifted her little sister's shoulders and head up off of the floor. With a few pats to the side of her little sister's face while asking if she was alright, it wasn't long until Jenna got a response. Just as Doodlebug told her that she thinks so, Jenna helped her up and led her to the couch.

Being more upset about having Drells blood running through her veins than having the blood over the stranger's, Doodlebug couldn't comprehend how that could be. Once Jenna got her little sister down on the couch she told her that they would get to the bottom of everything soon. After making sure her little sister was going to be alright, Jenna turned her attention back to Sal' Amanda.

As Sal' Amanda stood there starring at Jenna, she told her, "Truth may hurt but it's always worth knowing." Without saying anything to Sal' Amanda, Jenna just stood there starring at her just as her blood was ready to boil over. With a smile Jenna watched as Sal' Amanda removed the necklace that she wore. After she removed it from around her neck she tossed it out towards her just as a small winged demon made of black fire emerged and carried it on over. Just as the demon dropped it in the palm of Jenna's right hand the demon burnt out.

Right after the demon dropped the necklace off and Jenna was hold it in her hand, Sal' Amanda told her that it was for her little sister to wear, just as she told her all about it right after. Being a sliver of night which is a shield that can conceal one's own self and thoughts from all evil, the necklace is that. Just as the stone is an eye of her thoughts which can communicate to the thoughts of the wearer, whose thoughts may come questionable and will need guiding help to accomplish all which escapes. Just as it's a portal to hell for whoever wears it, besides who's chosen to. For as whoever wears it will be pulled in and fall to hell and only the one who's chosen to wear it will be able to save them.

While noticing that Doodlebug had drifted off to sleep there on the couch, Sal' Amanda looked towards her and told her, "Sleep is what you need because you like your sister are heading for something so dangerous, for either it could be deadly." After hearing that from Sal' Amanda, Jenna didn't hesitate to question her about that. Just as Sal' Amanda told Jenna that what she and her little sister are faced with isn't without danger for as it's with many, many in which could end their lively hood. While right after Sal' Amanda told her, "To name three, Makenzie, Gina and the faceless witch of Hades, but especially Makenzie if she succeeds in getting the witch's spell book, the Book of Dark"

After she told Jenna that, Sal' Amanda told her throughout their journey to save a princess's soul or to drive spirits or beings like the faceless witch back into the Book of Hearts comes many other dangers. Dangers great and small; dangers that are invisible to the eye but not to the mind; dangers of all kind. Dangers of deception, deceit and greed; dangers from your own self that you'll have to catch before you fall and even dangers from your little sister who soundly sleeps. Just as Sal' Amanda told Jenna, dangers she like her little sister will have to keep a close eye out for. Once Sal' Amanda finished, Jenna replied, "So what you're saying is for us to use common sense right." With a laugh, Sal' Amanda told her no not common sense but uncommon sense, a sense unknown to the average human, a sense in which surpasses all, a sense in which she and her little sister will have to learn to use before too long.

Right after she told that to Jenna, she looked at her and said, "Now I'll tell you what you must do. Just as she began by telling her that she first had to unlock the coffer, remove the fleece and unroll the Book of Hearts out from it. While after she must carefully unseal the princesses lock of hair from around the book and then open the book and start reading. When a story begins to be read no skimming through it or skipping to read about a different princess will the reader be able to do. For as unfinished stories will bleed on each page that the reader turns to and will begin where the reader left off at until the story has been completely read and an attempt has been made to save the soul of the princess.

Once a story has been read the reader must go seek out a place to break a calm pool of water, by a stick, a stone or by whatever is chosen. Like the calm hearts of the thirteen princesses which got broken and left them in tears, the water will break and form a funneling set of stairs. One thousand and thirteen steps to the funneling stairs the reader will have to travel up or down, with the last one leading to the place where the crown and gem of a princess can be found. The crown and gem which will save a princess's soul once found and placed on the Book of Hearts. Soon as the crown and gem is placed on top of the Book of Hearts a portion of the cover will vanish just like the pages of the story read about a princess and the hair and tears of that princess.

Before Jenna knew it, Sal' Amanda went, "POOF" right before her eyes just as she burned out without a trace of smoke. While being pretty sure of herself she could remember everything that she had to do, Jenna thought it would be for the best if she waited until her little sister and Podgy woke up before attempting to do anything. Just as the day was over and evening time had already begun she picked the coffer up from the floor and headed upstairs with it. While thereafter she headed for her bedroom to get a little rest.

Chapter Eight

What the Heck!

While a little rest wound out to be a good night's sleep, Jenna didn't wake up not until 2:30am the next morning. After waking up and heading down stairs with the coffer and necklace, she saw that her little sister and Podgy were up, just as they were sitting on the couch watching tv. Once she made it down the rest of the way she noticed that her little sister's hair was all in thin braids, similar to dreadlocks. Just as she approached the couch she asked her little sister what was up with the braids. While giving nothing less than a strange answer, Doodlebug told her since she was suppose to be a judge she thought she may as well have her hair braided up as one. Just as she told her that Sophie Sofasock stopped by and braided her hair up for her.

Sophie Sofasock was not what the sisters could call a friend or an enemy, for as was merely a once known field hockey player for the Greenground County Gators. Just as the sisters use to talk to her and her cousin Marie before and a little after they played against one another during their games during their high school years. While being twenty one years old and standing five foot five, Sophie had short black hair and sparkling navy-blue eyes just as she was a softly spoken female.

Giving Jenna a reason to smile and laugh a little, her little sister then handed her a belated birthday card that Sophie dropped off for her from her cousin Marie W. Marry. Just as the card was in a sealed white, red and pink hearted envelope, Jenna was somewhat surprised that her little sister didn't open it. While handing her little sister the necklace Sal' Amanda told her to wear, before doing anything else Jenna told her little sister everything that was told to her about it. Just as soon as Jenna finished, she made her way to the kitchen.

Marie W. Marry who lived in Greenground County and once played for the Gators had pretty much the same story with the sisters like her cousin Sophie. But unlike Sophie, Marie was given a nick name, "Hell's Heckler", by none other than Jenna. For as Marie was not only a top player for the Gators but she would always heckle at her opponents to where they would lose their concentration and she and her team mates could capitalize on their opponents mishaps. Just as she got under Jenna's skin many times by heckling. While looking nothing like her cousin Sophie, Marie looked allot like Baby Doll Stump. For as she had long strawberry red hair but curly instead of straight like Baby Doll's, she also had hazel eyes right along with a face wrecked with freckles. And like Baby Doll, Marie stood five foot four and was twenty four and a half years old.

Once Jenna made it into the kitchen she sat the coffer down on the table and pulled out a chair and sat down. While after running her fingernail across the top of the envelope she then pulled the birthday card out. With an outburst of laughter being let out, Jenna found much humor of the front of the card. For as it had a white duck, with "Happy Birthday", at the top and "Duck", below. After enjoying the picture she opened it up, just as this duck popped out with its bill open while a pink icing covered hockey puck with lit candles popped up and crammed into its bill causing the candles to fall over. Just as she closed the card a little and opened it a few times to watch as the hockey puck flew into the bill of the duck.

With more humor being found, a little bit more continued to be found when she read the inscription to the left side of the duck. Just as it read, "Duck, because that's no Birthday cake heading your way that's a hockey puck." After reading the card's inscription, Jenna saw an inscription on the other side done by Marie, just as she read it.

~

"At a Birthday age like you now are I hope I get to live to see"

"At a Birthday age of twenty five which is a year and a half ahead of me"

"It's something I'm hoping and praying for but I'll have to wait and see"

*"With time and this disease being my new opponent
it's going to be a challenge for me"*

*"I'm sure you've heard the rumors about what's
robbing my life that's unseen"*

*"Just as I'm sure you've heard that it's cancer but it's
not, it's something similar that's festering"*

*"While I sound greedy to bourdon my problems
on you just as we never were friends"*

*"Friends with you I would like to had been because
with friends there's a beginning and no end"*

*"Though with what we've been through on opposite
playing fields the other's face we seen"*

*"All of those moments you and I shared I never would trade in nor
would I ask for a different opposer than the four foot nine duckling"*

*"Ha, ha, hope you got a kick out of the duck within the card because
that's pretty well how you looked after our very first game"*

*"While with me being a Gator and you being a Orange Quacker
ha, ha, we may not had been friends but we weren't enemies
just opposing players who enjoyed field hockey the same"*

P.S.

~Happy Birthday Jenna, Hope you'll always remember me~

~Marie W. Marry~

After finishing, Jenna broke down in tears. While sitting there at the kitchen table crying, her sadness didn't go unnoticed for as her little sister and Podgy heard her crying. Just as they got up from the couch and headed to the kitchen it wasn't long until they found out what was going on. After Jenna told them and let them read the inscription in the card, Doodlebug became flabbergasted as to why Sophie didn't mention anything about her cousin's illness. Just as she told her sister that whatever Marie has, it sounds like the same thing that robbed Billbie's life away when they lived in Grimm Street. While Doodlebug never could figure Sophie out, she never could figure Marie out either.

Billbie Zilery was a childhood friend of the sisters when they lived in Grimm Street well before their parents passed away. Just as Billbie was like all of the other children who lived in Grimm Street he was being raised in poverty. While he like the rest of the children were good about sharing their toys with one another and looking out for each other there was one thing nobody could do for him when an illness fell upon him which took his life at the age of eight years old.

Once Doodlebug and Podgy got Jenna calm down, Doodlebug told her sister why not read from the Book of Hearts and get her mind off of everything else. After telling her sister that, Doodlebug laid the key to the coffer down in front of her sister. While picking up the key, Jenna took a moment to look at it. Once she finished, it took her four tries to get the coffer unlocked.

Just as the lid popped open, Jenna opened it the rest of the way while removing the book afterwards. After removing the book and carefully removing the lock of hair that kept it sealed, Jenna opened it up about three quarters away towards the end. Once she had the book opened and looked down towards the open pages, words bled right on them. Just as she turned and looked up at her little sister and asked with a wondrous tone in her voice, "Did you see that, Bug?" After asking Jenna remembered that only she and her twin could see the writing, just as she heard her little sister reply by asking, "See what sis?"

Right after Jenna explained to her little sister what happened, she turned her attention back to the Book of Hearts and started to read from it. While Podgy was sitting at the table across from her, Doodlebug pulled her out a chair and sat down at the other end in between her sister and Podgy. Just as Doodlebug sat there quietly facing towards the back door and the coat, hat rack which was nothing more than a full body female mannequin. A female mannequin which she had gotten from Mrs. Shanty a while back, which came from the old mannequin factory, "Manikin Ann's Mannequins", on Leg Alley in FallenForHer. Just as it was wearing her hat, vest and maze to my heart sunglasses that she stole, amongst other clothing.

~

"Hidden above the wondrous world and from all of those wondering souls"

"Was a kingdom hidden up in the white clouds,
a kingdom which was called Sole"

"While the Kingdom of Sole wasn't large like
those below but more so small"

"It was a very friendly kingdom that was all
up until thunder would start to roll"

"For as whenever the Kingdom of Sole quaked
as the cloud started to rumble"

"The people of the kingdom knew one thing that
they were heading for great trouble"

"Just as the sound of thunder become heard
the people would arm themselves"

"And take arm up against the anguipede army that
would come up from within the cloud"

"While the rumbling sound of rumbling thunder
was the kingdom's warning sound"

"*The sound always gave the people just enough
time to prepare for the coming battle*"

"*Once the once known white cloud turned gray
and lightening and rain below fell*"

"*Up through the cloud like snakes crawling out of
their holes the anguipede army welled*"

"*While some battles lasted for days, some lasted only for just a short while*"

"*Just as some battles weren't fought for months,
others were frequent and miserable*"

"*Just as long as the cloud of the Kingdom of
Sole stayed calm and white as snow*"

"*The anguipede army slept quite soundly while
without having any care in the world*"

"*But for the people of Sole, to be able to keep
the cloud calm and white as snow*"

"*Was simply impossible, for as the cloud which their
kingdom sat on they had no control*"

"*Just as the blood thirty anguipede army would
always blame being awaken on Sole*"

"*The Kingdom of Sole would always blame the
anguipede army for the cloud's control*"

"*While the control of the cloud's changes was
neither Sole's nor the anguipede faults*"

"*It never mattered for as when a storm was on the
verge to unfold the same story was told*"

"*Not only did rain fall down to the ground below
from the storm of the disturbed cloud*"

"*But so did many solders of the anguipede army
right along with quite a few people of Sole*"

~

"*With eyes blue as the evening sky and long
luscious soft hair white as snow*"

"*Princess Antoinette had the looks of an angle
and a heart which never grew cold*"

"*While being the sole survivor of her family
from battles that's now long gone*"

"*Princess Antoinette was just like her father and
mother very intelligent and strong*"

"*For as whenever a battle erupted she never
would let the Kingdom of Sole fall*"

"*Just as she always manage to drive the anguipede
army back down their snake holes*"

"*While the Kingdom of Sole was ran by Princess
Antoinette and no other soul*"

"*A day came when Princess Antoinette finally
met a prince, a prince named Lowell*"

"*Just as Prince Lowell had been kept hidden
there within the kingdom for so long*"

"He had been kept hidden for his safety and for
the kingdom to one day grow strong"

"From all eyes and even the princess's, Prince
Lowell grew at his parent's home"

"From all eyes of Sole, Prince Lowell grew until
he became old enough to be known"

"Daring, dashing and handsome; kind at heart
and polite also was Prince Lowell"

"Just as he was a long awaited answer of Princess
Antoinette's prayers and of Sole's"

"While having a heart of loneliness, to nobody
was the princess secret ever told"

"For as her secret stayed with her for an unknown
amount of time which was long"

"With her heart being filled and her secret
becoming forgotten for as it she let go"

"Princess Antoinette knew with Prince Lowell,
the Kingdom of Sole would never fall"

"While it was fate which brought together Princess
Antoinette and Prince Lowell"

"It would be fate which would separate them both
forever right before the fall of Sole"

"For as it was the day just before their wedding
as to when everything crumbled"

"Just as the sound of thunder started to rumble
it wasn't long till there came a battle"

"With the battle being huge and like no other,
the anguipede's target was Lowell"

"For as the prince, they knew they needed to get
rid of at all cost in order to conquer Sole"

~

"After the thunder came the cloud turned to gray
it soon turned black as pure coal"

"Just as thousands of anguipedes emerged up from
within and pounded the hell out of Sole"

"While the people of the kingdom of Sole didn't
back down from the horrific mulling"

"They fought right alongside Prince Lowell who
led them and led the charge of the battle"

"With the battle being so fierce it was the most
brutal one that anyone had ever saw"

"For as the sky rain with bodies, blood, and heads
of both anguipedes and people of Sole"

~

After finishing the first paragraph of the third page, Jenna noticed that the lock of hair was gone. While laying the Book of Hearts down she saw her little sister heading over towards the mannequin with the lock of hair. Just as she asked her little sister what in the world she was doing, her little sister simply told her that she just wanted to see something. Having little less than no concern, Jenna told her to be careful with the lock of hair.

While Jenna watched on like Podgy, they watched as Doodlebug tilted the hat sideways that the mannequin was wearing and placed an end of the lock of hair up against the side of the it's bald head. Just as she turned slightly and looked back she asked her sister, "You think she'd look nice with a wig this color sis?" Before Jenna had a chance to answer, she started to see hair sprout out from the side of the mannequin's head. While blasting up from her chair just as it fell over backwards behind her, Jenna pointed towards the mannequin and yelled, "Bug watch out."

Becoming clueless of what her sister was yapping about, just as Doodlebug was about to drop her hand from the side of the mannequin's head she soon got a shock of her life. Just as her hand wouldn't drop down, Doodlebug got a weird look on her face just as she said, "What the heck", while turning back towards the mannequin afterwards. Just as soon as she got turned, her jaw dropped and her eyes grew big. While not only seeing that the lock of hair had taken hold to the side of the mannequin's head but she saw hair the same colors as the lock growing out from around it.

Just as Doodlebug let go of the lock of hair she stumbled backwards while bumping into the table. While the mannequin's head quickly filled up with hair the body from head to toe started to change from hard plastic to fleshy human skin. Just as Doodlebug was speechless she also became frozen in place. Like Doodlebug, so was her sister and Podgy as they looked on.

As the plastic formed to skin, the mannequin slowly started to move a little. While the plastic was taking form, the painted hazel plastic eyes were taking true form as well. Just as the mannequin's lips broke open, the mannequin said "I'm human again", just as it had a young female voice. After it was in human form, the mannequin looked straight at Doodlebug and asked her, "Who are you."

After hearing that Doodlebug stuttered out a short laugh right before she fell to the floor from fainting, just as Podgy followed right after. Right after Doodlebug and Podgy fainted, the mannequin looked straight at Jenna right before taking off through the kitchen.

Just as the mannequin ran right over top of Podgy, the mannequin ran right on into the living room. While Jenna followed just as she was yelling for the mannequin to stop, she caught her right before she was about to crash through a window.

Once Jenna stopped the mannequin and got her to turn around towards her, she asked what her name was. Just as the mannequin looked dead eye at Jenna, she told her that her name was Breanna a younger sister to Princess Miranda. While afterwards Breanna asked Jenna who she was, she then asked where in the world was she at. Once Jenna answered Breanna's questions she told her about everything else. After gaining Breanna's trust not to run away she led her back into the kitchen and introduced her to her little sister and Podgy after waking both of them up.

CHAPTER NINE

Start

KALEIDOSCOPE COVE

With all Jenna told Breanna plus all that her little sister and Podgy told her, she realized that the modern world that she was now in, she wouldn't survive for very long without friends. Just as she was a living human being once again who could get hurt or even killed. While with a couple of days passing by as she became dégagé, it didn't take Breanna very long to acquire an appetite for modern food and acquired an appetite for modern clothing too which the sisters had something to do with. Just as they showed Breanna all throughout Foot County while showing her a good time, they like she felt like they've been friends forever.

Like Jenna, Doodlebug knew she would have to get Breanna back into the Book of Hearts. While not being too enthused to do so, Doodlebug thought if her sister didn't mention it and they kept her out of Sal' Amanda's sight she wouldn't have to worry about it for a while. Just like Jenna, Doodlebug was becoming very fond of Breanna, for as they both thought of her more as a sister than a friend. With the passing of a week Jenna thought that it was time to open the Book of Hearts and finish where she left off at.

While everybody found a place at the kitchen table, Podgy sitting across from Jenna and Breanna sitting across from Doodlebug, the table became full. Just as Jenna unlocked the coffer and removed the book, she ran her finger around where the lock of hair should had been just as she looked over at her little sister. While Doodlebug shrugged her shoulders and raised her eyebrows without asking her sister what, Doodlebug knew that she wouldn't be able to send Breanna back. After seeing her little sister's reaction Jenna, turned her head, opened the Book of Hearts and started to read.

~

*"While Princess Antoinette watched the horrific
battle from the princess tower of the castle"*

*"Near the battle's end there came a scene which broke
her heart just as she cried out Lowell"*

"*Just as she watch as he and this anguipede that
he was fighting with took a deadly fall*"

"*Not to the ground of the cloud but right off it and
down to the unforgiving ground below*"

"*Little after Prince Lowell had fallen to his death;
there soon came the end of the battle*"

"*For as it came at a high cost, the cost of the prince
and three fourths of the people of Sole*"

"*Just as days slowly turned into weeks and
then months started to quickly fall*"

"*Princess Antoinette rarely was seen roaming
about in public of the kingdom of Sole*"

"*With a broken heart and a grieving soul, on
the princess it was taking a great toll*"

"*For as Princess Antoinette couldn't find any
hope what so ever for her to even hold*"

"*While keeping herself away from the public
and hidden in a place dark and cold*"

"*She kept herself hidden down in the empty
dungeon right there in the castle of Sole*"

"*While she was being held captive and as a
prisoner to her very own sorrows*"

"*The moment when she thought for sure that
all was lost, a voice of hope called*"

"A voice of a male which called out told her, I can right all of what's wrong"

*"I can get rid of the anguipedes and bring back
Prince Lowell and restore Sole"*

"Just as a light emerged it broke not only the darkness but it broke the cold"

*"Just as a stranger was reviled to a tearful Princess
Antoinette who was humbled"*

~

*"After reviling himself to Princess Antoinette
to him she said, that's impossible"*

*"Just as she told him all that he told her is
impossible and that he really should go"*

*"While not being persistent he told her that he
would go only if again he's told"*

*"Just as he told her one more chance he wanted
to give, for as the future he'd show"*

*"Without a word to say to him, Princess
Antoinette watched as an image arose"*

*"From out of the stranger's hands came a scene
Princess Antoinette had always hoped"*

*"While viewing the scene, Princess Antoinette
saw people cheering there in Sole"*

*"People who had lost their lives fighting against
the anguipede army in the last battle"*

"*Just as they with others were happily cheering
there right in front of the castle*"

"*Princess Antoinette was able to tell that they
were all quite a few years older as well*"

"*While she listened to their cheers she heard,
hail to the new prince, Prince Saul*"

"*Just as the scene of the image showed her holding
a child while standing beside Lowell*"

"*After seeing that Princess Antoinette looked
at the stranger and asked him how*"

"*Seeing a look of hope on her face the stranger
replied, no not how, what about now*"

"*What about telling me that's what you want,
so for you, with that I can help out*"

"*Just as she told the stranger that was what she
wanted and she wanted it right now*"

"*Once he had her right where he wanted her the
stranger looked at her and smiled*"

"*Right after he told her a promise she would have
to keep before that life can be found*"

"*While asking what the promise was that she
would have to keep was about*"

"*The stranger told her the promise would be a
task which she'd have to venture out*"

*"A task that would make since to her and all
of us, a task of Sole's head count"*

*"A count of all who is alive in the kingdom
besides any anguipede or any animals"*

*"Afterwards, once she told him the correct number
then all hope would be found"*

*"All which she saw in the image plus more, she
would receive within a second of an hour"*

~

*"After the stranger told her that, Princess
Antoinette told him she'd start now"*

*"Being eager to start, the stranger told her there's
more before she decides to go out"*

*"Just as he told her if she chose to accept and
failed, to him she'd lose her soul"*

*"But if she chose not to accept than from her and
the kingdom of Sole he would go"*

*"Just he told her that the choice was for her to
make which by her can be told"*

*"Just as he told her what she could gain, "Lowell"
and what she could lose, her soul"*

*"Having no doubt that she would successfully
succeed, yes became her answering call"*

*"Just as she told him that it was just yesterday she
went out and took a head count of Sole"*

*"As a huge smile grew on the stranger's face he
told her, well then why not tell us all"*

*"With a smile on her face, Princess Antoinette told
him five hundred and fourteen in all"*

*"Just as she told him that was counting her own
self and the new born she got to hold"*

*"While the smile stayed on the stranger's face, he shook
his head and told her that she was wrong"*

*"Just as the smile fell from Princess Antoinette,
she uttered wrong that's impossible"*

*"While afterwards he told her, yes if it were
yesterday her count would be correctly so"*

*"But yesterday isn't today princess and yesterday
I wasn't in the Kingdom of Sole"*

*"Unlike today which I now am just as my head
wasn't counted by one like one was told"*

*"After hearing that Princess Antoinette slapped
him hard as tears started to roll"*

*"Just as she screamed at him and told him to
leave from her kingdom and go home"*

*"With a careless laugh the stranger told Princess
Antoinette not without her soul"*

*"Just as he then told her that she knew all that
was at stake and that he's not at fault"*

*"While afterwards he told her, without her
around, her kingdom will finally fall"*

*"Without her around, the rest of her people will
parish and not by age of growing old"*

*"Before Princess Antoinette had a chance to say
anything to the ground she fell cold"*

*"For as her soul left from her body and went to the
stranger who afterwards left from Sole"*

~

*"The crown of clouds and the diamond heart shape
gem are still in the Kingdom of Sole"*

*"Right there in the castle hidden from the anguipedes
who for, searches when thunder rolls"*

*"While the only time that's safe to search for them
is when the cloud is white as snow"*

*"For as when awaken a anguipede can sniff out the
scent of human like a pack of wolvid dogs"*

*"While the anguipedes are a great danger other
dangers also lie within the castle walls"*

*"Dangers which were place there to protect Princess
Antoinette from anything and from all"*

~

Just as the story about Princess Antoinette came to an end Jenna
closed up the Book of Hearts and told everybody that it was gear
rounding up time. But before everybody got up from the table they
took the time to figure out what they might need. Once they had

a list made they went out and searched throughout the house for everything. While afterwards they loaded up, "Bucket of Rust and Bolts", Jenna's station wagon and headed to a Kaleidoscope Cove which was a secluded cove at Her Lake.

Not only did Lake Her sit in the suburb of Her but Her Dam which form the lake and was built on the FallenForHer River sat three fours of a mile above the prism and the prism bars. With the lake having many coves, Kaleidoscope Cove had only parking place and to get it you had to climb down a pathless hillside through briars and woods. While knowing that it was a scenic destination for boaters who love the autumn view just as the colorful leaves would reflect down onto the water beautifully when calm, Jenna also knew that boaters rarely ran through there during night.

Once they made it to Kaleidoscope Cove and pulled in the parking place they all got out and unloaded what little they were taking. While being late evening, there was about an hour of daylight left. Just as they made their way down over the hill it took them little over thirty minutes to get to the cove's end. Once they made it down they got a beautiful eye view. Just as they were looking out through the cove towards the open lake, they saw the sun just as it was starting to set over a hill. While being a deep mellow reddish-orange color, the color reflected down throughout the middle of the cove just as the colorful autumn leaves on the trees reflected down along the sides of it.

CHAPTER TEN

Start

THE KINGDOM OF SOLE

While the four took the opportunity to admire the view, they done so without seen any boats around. Just as soon as the sun fell away, Jenna turned her attention towards the water just as she asked herself how in the world was she going to get it to break. While asking herself that as she nicked the water's top with the putting end of her field hockey stick, Jenna soon got her answer. Right after the end of her field hockey stick stuck the water, from the water's top, tear drops began descending up towards this white cloud hovering above. While the tear drops numbers grew and grew all eyes became glued on the scene.

Just as they watched as the tear drops quickly started to take form, it wasn't too long until there was a spiraling stairway to the white cloud. With the cove looking the same, it looked as if not a drop of water was taken from it. While the first step began at the water's edge near where she struck it; it like the rest were as clear with a light bluish tent. Just as Jenna looked at everyone, she told them that it was go time.

With the stairway looking less than being steep as they spiraled up like a lock of hair, it was the steps which were the problem of concern for as they were right at eight foot wide. While Jenna had a coil of climbing rope strung down over her right shoulder and down under her left arm, she also had her field hockey stick there in her right hand. Just as she started up, Breanna soon followed, just as she had a backpack filled with a few things which they may need along with the Book of Hearts. After Breanna started up Doodlebug followed behind her. Just as she was wearing the hat and vest she had stolen along with the sandal while carrying a slingshot her dad had made for her a long time ago, a double shooter. Once she started up Podgy shortly followed, just as he had on a back pack filled with other things that they thought they might need.

Once they all were well on their way it didn't take them very long to figure out with every step they took it was like taking five at a time. While the steps escalated beneath their feet only when they took steps, whenever they stopped the water stayed still just as they found out. Just as Breanna ran right into Jenna the first time she stopped and looked back to check on everybody, while Podgy ran right into Doodlebug when she stopped to check on him. While the higher they got the lighter they and their stomachs felt and the narrower the steps seem to be. With panic setting in only once for Doodlebug the moment she was halfway up and decided to look straight down, the rest of the way up went almost like a breeze.

Little after they entered through the bottom of the cloud it wasn't long until disturbance filled their eyes along with their minds. The moment they were halfway through the cloud they came upon a huge tunnel six times their height. While doing the unthinkable which one couldn't possibly imagine, instead of moving on up the steps Jenna stepped off from them and headed down the tunnel a short ways. Just as the others done the same just as they followed her lead, the moment Podgy stepped off from the stairs it collapsed and came crashing down from where it came. With a troublesome sound that the stairs made as they fell, it grabbed all of their attentions and caused them to turn around and rush back. After Podgy told them what happened they knew they were heading straight for trouble.

Little after the collapse of the stairs they all thought it would be wise to stay as close as possible, just as they started down the tunnel. As a light breeze was felt flowing from within the tunnel it was quite graveolent. Just as there was such a dreadful stench which it was carrying. While the breeze stayed the same the stench grew stronger and stronger the further they went in. For as the stench which they were inhaling had a smell of ten thousand rotten eggs mixed with ten thousand rotting dead rats.

With flashlights all on as they were making their way through the darkness of the tunnel, it wasn't long until it came to an end which ended at a large room. Just as it looked to be empty that was minus the stench, they slowly made their way on through to one of the two tunnels which ran out from its sides. With the right tunnel being their choice, the moment Jenna and Breanna entered in, wind from their movement whirled up around and swooped off a little of the cloud from the wall's side of the room.

Just as Doodlebug was about to enter in, she espied these four dark dingy green scaly limbs which were along the wall's side. While they quickly became submerged back in the cloud within a split second after catching her eyes, the first thought she had was, was she just seeing things or what. Just as she started fanning her hands back and forth out in front of her, Podgy with a laugh told her all that fanning isn't going to do much good. Before she had a chance to tell him what she was doing, what she had thought she had seen became reviled again. Without having to say anything to Podgy, he became stunned from what she uncovered. Just as he told her, "I heard of a snake in the grass but never a snake in the cloud", she told him to get down below her and help her to create more wind so they can see more.

As the two got busy and started working together it wasn't long until four sleeping snake limbs became uncovered. Just as the snake heads of the ends of the limbs were as big as or a little bigger than Doodlebug's head, they were also pretty much alive at that. While realizing they uncovered a lower part of an anguipede, Doodlebug told Podgy to stay put while she goes and gets her sister. Doing like she asked, Podgy watched as she took off down the tunnel.

While Doodlebug flew down the tunnel, the moment she came upon her sister and Breanna she gave a whispering shout at them. After getting their attention she motioned for them to come back, just as she quickly turned back around and headed back to where she left Podgy at. Just as soon as everybody made it to where Podgy was at, Doodlebug first told her sister and Breanna what happened while afterwards she and Podgy showed them. After she and Podgy showed Jenna and Breanna the snake limbs, Doodlebug told them that it's hard to tell what's hidden throughout the cloud walls. While right afterwards she told them if it starts to storm they're in for some serious trouble.

After reviling her find to her sister, Doodlebug found herself doing allot more fanning. Just as she, her sister, Breanna and Podgy created a wind storm with their hands, more and more that was hidden within the cloud became reviled. While more and more sleeping snake headed limbs were uncovered so was this platform which the anguipedes were sitting on. Just as they found a space in between two of the anguipedes there on the platform big enough for all four of them plus one or two more, Jenna had her little sister, Breanna and Podgy to boost her up. For as she wanted to try to get a look at what the rest of the anguipedes looked like.

Just as the platform was a tad over six foot tall, the height didn't stop her from getting up there for as her determination and help from her little sister and friends conquered it. Once she made it up, she had to keep fanning her hands around to work away the cloud. While getting down on her hands and knees she told them she'd drop down the rope so they could climb up. After dropping the rope down it wasn't long until everybody made it up.

Once they got situated around and were facing the same direction they started fanning the cloud from one of the anguipedes. While uncovering hands, forearms, stomach and the waist the human portion of the anguipede had a reddish brown tint to it. Just as the anguipede wore a short leather-ish looking gladiator kilt around its waist, it also wore wide steel cuffs around its wrist. With the cloud being such a pain to cope with, Jenna asked Podgy if he could lift her up on his shoulders long enough for her to see if she could create enough wind to get a look at the anguipede's face.

Having no problem with what Jenna wanted him to do; Podgy squatted down and told her whenever she's ready. While telling her little sister and Breanna once she was up for them to start fanning out in front of Podgy so he wouldn't become disoriented from not being able to see, they told her sure thing. Once Podgy had Jenna lifted up on his shoulders they heard Doodlebug ask herself, "What in the world did I roll over." Just as she bent over and started fanning her hand while shinning her flashlight down towards what she rolled over, she let out a uh-oh.

After hearing her say uh-oh, Jenna asked her what was wrong. Just as Doodlebug told her sister that she accidently rolling over top of the fingers of one of the anguipedes, all at once a whoosh sound was heard. While right afterwards a tongue came rolling down over the top of her hat and down in front of her face while flickering at the others. Just as Jenna told her little sister to stay calm and not to move and everything would be alright, up from above Doodlebug came a gust of wind blowing down on her. With the wind knocking out a huge patch of the cloud, behind it as it was blowing came this hideous looking male face.

Sort of like a human male's face the face of the anguipede was, just as it was much larger but shaped the same. With slender thick pointed ears and a wide ridged stubby four nostril nose, like human he also looked to be part hog. While the skin of his face was reddish-brown, his lips were thin and skimpy just as they were black as coal. Just as his eyes were balls of white with pitch black pupils which were curvy four pointed stars, the anguipede also had teeth like a carcajou. With long brittle yellowish-white hair and a serpent forked tongue the anguipede male was a sight which would make one wish they were blind.

With a small laugh Doodlebug told her sister, she has nothing to worry about, just as she held out the stone amulet of her necklace and said, "Remember sis what Sal' Amanda told you." While seeing a disturb look on her sister's face, Doodlebug questioned her about the necklace, about it supposing to hide her from all evil. While Jenna had to break the bad news to her little sister about the difference between evil and mythological beings, she also had to break away from Podgy and help her out so she wouldn't get eaten. Right after Jenna told her little sister the difference, Doodlebug muttered loudly, "The anguipedes are not evil but mythological what, the anguipedes are not evil but mythological WHAT."

Just as Jenna leaped from Podgy and drove her field hockey stick on top of the head of the snake, it dropped like a ton of bricks. While Doodlebug moved out of the way seconds before her sister collided with the head of the snake, she moved out of the way only to get a frightening view of the human face of the anguipede and his hands that were heading her way. Just as she heard the anguipede say, "I smell the blood of a human." With everything happing so fast, Doodlebug dropped her flashlight, pulled out her double-shot slingshot from her vest pocket along with two steel balls and told him, "You forgot to say fee-fi-foe-fumb you big nasty looking dumb-dumb." Just as she shot him point blank in the face.

With one of the steel balls striking the anguipede right in between his eyes, the other one hit him right on his forehead. While the anguipede swung his hands up to his face cutting two huge slashes through the cloud, it wasn't long afterwards till he fell sideways into the other anguipede. Just as he like his one snake limb became knocked out, Jenna, Doodlebug, Breanna and Podgy wasted no time in getting down from the platform. While hoping none of the others became woken, they stuck around for a short while to see.

While they stood there waiting to see if any became woken, Jenna told them that there has to be a way up to the cloud's top if not many ways. Just as she reminded them about what the Book of Hearts said about the anguipedes coming up from the cloud, she told them one of those ways they need to find. Right after telling them that, from within the cloud and throughout the platform the sound of movement started to be heard. While not sticking around to find out what becomes of the sound, all four quickly took off down the tunnel to the right.

After taking off down the tunnel it wasn't long until they came upon what looked to be a way out. With a towering chamber being found which had a long wide swirl of cloud going straight up, Jenna was sure of herself hidden beneath the cloud was a set of steps. While shinning her flashlight down where the swirl started, Jenna started to move towards it. Just as she kept moving she soon found out that there weren't any steps but there was solid ground beneath her feet leading up. With an outer wall hidden behind the cloud and emptiness in the center it wasn't long until all four of them were heading up.

With the hike up around the swirl being paved with not only holes and stones, it also had its fare share of human bones. Once the four made it to the end they stood together and upheaved on the stone-like object which had the hole covered. While taking all of what they had to get the object to move, the moment they did, they soon found their selves there in the once known Kingdom of Sole. With the ruins of homes that the people once lived in being seen scattered all around, in the far distance the castle of Sole became seen standing ragged and tall there beneath a blood moon.

CHAPTER ELEVEN

Start

TRIPPIN WITH TRAPS

Once they covered the hole back up with the stone, they headed straight for the castle of Sole. While the ground was cloud covered about three foot, they knew anything could happen along the way. They could trip over something and fall; they could step on something such as a nail or get their foot caught or they could simply fall straight down into one of the anguipede holes. With the distance to the castle being about a half mile all of them crossed their fingers hoping nothing along the way would go wrong. Just as the four walked side to side heading for the castle, Jenna asked Breanna where might a princess hide her crown and gem at. With a point of a finger, Breanna told her defiantly not in a princess tower.

While the princess tower was a thought that crossed her mind just like it was in her sight, Jenna thought that for most it might be too obvious but being too obvious might be the prime place for them to start their search. Just as they were gaining ground and coming closer to the castle, Breanna went on and told Jenna defiantly not under the throne of her mother and father either but where she perished there in the dungeon. After hearing that Jenna looked at her and told her with that being the best place to search out, that would be where they would head to first. With many disturbing crackling and crunching sounds being heard along the way beneath their feet, there came one which braked Doodlebug's wheel from moving.

Soon after a crunch followed by a ka-thoop sound was heard, Doodlebug just about fell face first to the unseen ground. While catching herself before letting it happen, it didn't take her very long to find out what it was that she ran over. Just as she lifted her left leg up and looked behind, there stuck on her wheel was a human skull. For as the skull which she had rolled over, it was laying on its side while facing her oncoming. While missing the mouth, she rolled right over the nose and eyes just her wheel fell down through the top and became stuck. With a sarcastic, "Great", being let out after seeing what it was that braked her wheel from moving, Doodlebug had Podgy to remove it for her.

Little after the removal of the skull they arrived at the castle's gates. Just as they were constructed of wood with lunette tops, their tops together curved like a rainbow. While the gates were at lease fifteen feet tall, the two statues which stood at each side were about five feet taller. For as there were these two gigantic guardian winged angels with shield and sword in striking position at each side guarding the gates. With intimidating looks, the angels were quite intimidating to Jenna, Doodlebug, Breanna and Podgy.

Just as it took all four of them to push open the gates, two on one side and two on the other. It didn't take them long to walk fifty yards afterwards to the castle steps. While it looked like there were about a hundred to a hundred and fifty steps to the castle's entry, the steps were roughly thirty feet wide just as they curved like the crescent of the moon. Just as they started up the steps it wasn't long until they were pushing the doors to the castle open.

Like the gates, the doors to the castle were also doubled and curved at the top. While like the gates, it also took all four of them to push them open. Once they had the doors pushed open they flickered their flashlights around as they slowly entered in. While the floor was thickly covered with cloud dust, it was quiet easy to tell that the anguipedes had previously been throughout the castle. For as it was easy to see all of the slithering snake trails going every which way.

While the room they entered into was quite large approximately forty squared foot, off to each sides were two passage ways while straight out in front of them was a short flight of steps. Just as the flight of steps were identical to those which led up to the castle, there were little less of them though for as there were only thirty of them. While the walls were bare of material things, only the stones and the mortar were seen. With many choices to choose from it was a tad mind boggling to figure out which way be the most logical for them to go. While standing there looking around, Jenna asked Breanna if she knew which way would lead them down to the dungeon. Without questioning herself, Breanna replied and told Jenna in order to get to the dungeon at her father's palace one had to go up before going down to it, just as she pointed up towards the top of the steps. After hearing that from Breanna, Jenna told everybody that was where they were going to go first.

Before they started for the steps, Doodlebug asked her sister if booby traps were evil. With a hard to answer question, Jenna told her yes and no that it could go both ways. Just as she told her little sister if a booby trap was made from evil she shouldn't have anything to worry about but if a booby trap is made by a princess or one who is not evil then she probably wouldn't be safe from any of them. After explaining her answer to her little sister they headed for the flight of steps.

Once they made it up the flight of steps out to each side was a passage way. Just as the one to the right curved forward, the one to the left curved back towards the entrance way of the castle. While looking back and forth at them, Breanna told Jenna, one should lead to the throne room and the other should lead down to the dungeon. Just as she told her, to the right should lead to the throne room and the one to the left should lead down to the dungeon.

With four people and two ways to go, Jenna thought they could cover more ground if they split up into two groups. After talking it over with everybody and after everybody agreed that it was a good idea they split up into two groups. While Doodlebug and Podgy took off they headed for the right passage way, Jenna and Breanna done the same just as they headed for the left passage way. Just as both ways had slithering snake trails on the floor.

After the groups headed around the passage ways, Doodlebug and Podgy had a short walk just as the passage way was right at twenty yards and ended at the throne room to the left. Just as the throne room was humongous; it had plenty enough room for the royalties to be entertained. While the throne room had already been ransacked a dozen times over, Doodlebug and Podgy did see the thrones of the princess's mother and father. For as both were toppled over just as one was laying at one end of the room while the other was laying near the center of the room.

Just as they saw the thrones they also saw where they had once sat, just as there was a large hiding place big enough for at least four grown people to hide in. While shinning their flashlights down in the hiding place they saw nothing but emptiness. Like the hiding place, the throne room was empty beside the thrones, the hiding place and this passageway back behind where the thrones use to sit. Just as they made their way to the passageway, it wasn't long until they saw the corpse of an anguipede.

Bones sheeted with torn dried skin, a bag of bones covering a large section of the passageway's floor. Just as the corpse of an anguipede held in his right hand this three pointed pitchfork which had an eight foot long wooden handle, the points of it were right at three foot. While the two outer points bowed out before curving in and coming to a point, the one in the middle was straight. With caution as Doodlebug and Podgy slowly crept down the passageway to the corpse, she told him that the anguipede must have set off a trap which killed him.

Once they made it to the snake heads of the limbs of the anguipede, Podgy flashed his light on the corpse just as Doodlebug flashed hers all around the ceiling, floor and walls. After seeing four two inch sizes holes three feet apart and in a diamond form along the right side of the wall, she saw the same on the left side but instead of a diamond form they were in the form of a square. With the hole sets being right across from each other, Doodlebug pointed them out to Podgy before telling him to step back three or four feet. Just as soon as Podgy done as she asked, Doodlebug squatted down, grabbed the end of the pitchfork handle and pulled back on it. With the weight of pitchfork dragging heavily back across the floor while a large portion of the corpse moved back with it, it didn't take long until the trap was set off.

With a blisting sound shredding the air, with it were these eight noodle shaped stone spears which had jagged shearing edges frontwards and backwards right along with pointed ends. While as fast as they came out, they went back in just as fast. After setting off the trap just as it scared Doodlebug causing her to fall backwards on her butt, she slightly turned halfway around and looked back at Podgy. While wearing a huge smile just as she ran the back of her left hand across her forehead, she let out a, "W-ow-ch", and laughed a little. Once her silliness came to an end she told him that she hopes he's not scared to do a little crawling because that's what they're going to have to do.

While the lowest hole which housed a deadly spear was about two and a half feet from the floor, Doodlebug knew they shouldn't have any problems crawling beneath it. Before they started under they took the time to pull the corpse of an anguipede back and lay it long ways from end to end of the walls. Just as Doodlebug wrote, "Booby trap sis ahead", on the floor in the thick cloud dust right behind the corpse just in case her sister and Breanna came searching for her and Podgy. With the movement of the corpse setting off the trap quite a few times, Doodlebug knew that it was bound to go off when she and Podgy started under.

Once the way was clear for them to crawl under Doodlebug went first. Just as soon as she came upon the center of the spear trap, the blisting sound of air being sheared was heard right above her head. Just as the bottom spear nicked the top of her hat, she dropped her head as far as she could to the floor. With her chin touching the floor and her eyes looking straight forward the moment she started moving again off went the trap. Having no intentions to stop, she became a little careless from becoming scared. Just as she turned her wheel upward so it could roll, it wasn't long until it got stuck twice, through the tire and through the rim.

Right after she made it safely through she told Podgy to stay flat on the floor and crawl like a snail. Doing like she told him, Podgy started under while forgetting to remove his backpack. While once he came upon the center of the trap it went off just as one of the spears went through the top of his backpack right behind his neck. With the air shredding sound being quite terrifying, Podgy tried to scuffle on through quickly. Just as the trap got set off several times, by the time Podgy made it safely through his backpack looked like Swiss cheese for as it was full of holes.

With a busted tire and rim, Doodlebug didn't waste time dwelling on it for as right after she made sure Podgy was alright they took off on through the passageway. While that part of the passageway was without any snake tracks, it wasn't without more traps. Just as they kept a sharp eye out for holes in the walls, ceiling and floor, they weren't ready for an unseen trap. For as once they made it about ten yards from the first trap, the floor beneath them caved in. While becoming trapped in a pit that was approximately twelve foot high with walls that weren't straight up and down but were like a volcano, they knew it was impossible to climb out but not impossible to get out.

Being handed a challenge to try to overcome like the pit that they were stuck in, Doodlebug and Podgy didn't seem to be having it as lucky as Jenna and Breanna were. For as the passageway they took was short and sweet, three yards and two feet long just as it led to two short flights of steps leading down to a caved-in room believed to be the dungeon. While within the rubble there were the remnants of a not so lucky anguipede. With the room being unsearchable they turned around and headed back out of the passageway.

Soon after they made it out of the passageway it wasn't long until they were heading into the one Doodlebug and Podgy took. Just as soon as they came upon the anguipede corpse and read the writing there on the floor, they heard Doodlebug call out, don't walk any further it's a trap. With a light shinning zigzag-idly towards them from the far, all they were able to see was Doodlebug's head and arms poking up from the floor.

Just as they watched as she pulled herself on up and out, it wasn't long afterwards till she made her way to where they were, that was right across from them on the other side of the spear trap. While after showing them the holes and telling them what comes out of them and what they can do just as she pointed at her wheel, she clued them in on how to go about getting passed them. Once she knew her sister and Breanna were pretty much out of harm's way she hurried back to the pit and told Podgy help was on the way. Once Jenna and Breanna made it safely passed the spear trap, it wasn't long afterwards till she dropped down the rope for Podgy to climb up.

While Jenna, Doodlebug and Breanna held on the rope as he climbed up it, Jenna asked her little sister how in the world did she manage to get out like she did. Just as Doodlebug told her that with a few of the stone that fell with them, they piled up a few in the form of steps and then she had Podgy to lift her up onto his shoulders. After hearing her little sister's answer just as Podgy was on the verge of being out, Jenna asked her one other question. For as Jenna's question was, if she had any suggestions on how they could make it across the pit so they could see where the passageway leads to.

Right after Podgy made it out, without saying anything besides a tap to the side of her head while wearing brilliant look on her face Doodlebug took off back towards the spear trap. While after a minute or two there she came back just as she was lugging on the pitchfork of the anguipede. Once she made it back she told her sister all they have to do is lay the pitchfork across the hole of the pit and then shimmy their selves across. Just as she told her sister that's the only way she knows.

Setting the sail to her little sister's idea which was the only one they had, after they laid the pitchfork across the hole of the pit, Jenna handed Breanna her field hockey stick and sailed across. While hanging upside down just as she held on by wrapping her lower legs around the staff of the pitchfork, she pulled herself right along with the use of her hands. Just as she was making time good getting across, the others kept their flashlights pointed towards her so she could see. Once she made it across she told Breanna to toss over her field hockey stick and then the backpacks.

Doing like she was asked, Breanna tossed over her field hockey stick. While removing her backpack right afterwards, Doodlebug told her to go ahead and cross and she would have Podgy to toss over the two backpacks. Right after handing Doodlebug the backpack, it didn't take Breanna very long to make it across. Just as soon as Breanna made it across, Doodlebug had Podgy to toss over both of the backpacks. Once the backpacks were across Doodlebug told Podgy that it was his turn to cross.

Once everybody made it across and removed the pitchfork from the hole, Doodlebug and Podgy held to the handle's end of it and pushed it forwards back and forth across the floor. With the idea of using the pitchfork the way they were, it was in case if there were any other traps they would become sprung beforehand instead of when it would be too late. While Doodlebug and Podgy swept the floor, Jenna and Breanna combed the ceiling, walls and even the floor for booby-trap signs with their flashlights. Just as they were working together while moving slowly forward, the moment they saw the passageway's end which ended at an entranceway to a room they watched as some of the floor started to give away and fall.

While coming to a heart stopping halt, Doodlebug and Podgy quickly pulled back on the pitchfork so they wouldn't lose it. Just as Doodlebug bellowed out, "Dag on this place is trippin with traps", her sister replied, "Yeah why don't you tell me about it." After Jenna's reply to her little sister, Breanna told them that, "If fear of becoming conquered, the last resort for most all kingdoms is to set all of the traps." Just as she went on and told them, "But to find the device or whatever sets and unsets them it would be like trying to find a needle in a hay stack on the count they're usually well hidden." With part of the floor falling away, Jenna and Breanna shined their flashlights down to where it fell. While seeing a twelve foot drop, right along with a treacherous ground below covered with motley size coned stone spikes, Jenna told her little sister and Podgy to move the pitchfork around more over some more of the floor. Just as Doodlebug and Podgy moved the pitchfork across more of the floor more gave away and fell.

Just as ninety-eight percent of the floor fell from where they ran the pitchfork over only two percent stayed up. With a foot wide path becoming uncovered as they ran the pitchfork across more and more of the floor, the path which was becoming uncovered was anything but straight. For as it was a whole lot more curvy than any snake could possibly make. Once they were out of reach of the rest of the floor besides venturing down the exposed path, Jenna told her little sister that she would swop places with her. While Jenna and Podgy started down the path with the pitchfork, Doodlebug and Breanna followed while providing them light to see where they were going.

Little after they started down the path and came in contact with the rest of the floor, more and more gave away and fell while more and more of the path became uncovered. Just as more and more of the path became uncovered, more and more of a challenge the path became. From a single windy foot wide path to a single windy foot wide broken up path where stones grew further and further apart, the leaps to stone to stone weren't for the faint of heart. With the task being anything but easy, their minds became eased the moment that the end of the path to the passageway came and they entered into the room.

CHAPTER TWELVE

Start

CROWN AND GEM OF
PRINCESS ANTOINETTE

W himsical were the words that could only describe the looks on Jenna's, Doodlebug's and Podgy's faces the moment they saw what was there in the room. As a brilliant white glow engulfed the room from the light of their flashlights shining on a huge mound of different size coins there in front of them, all they were able to think was wow. While the three were in a daze, Breanna had to get them back to reality. Just as she put a hand on Jenna's shoulder and a hand on Doodlebug's shoulder and shook them a little while asking if they were ok, she then done the same to Podgy after the sisters came through.

Once Breanna got them back to reality, they made their way to the mound of coins. Just as Jenna scooped up half of a handful, she came to realizing that they weren't ordinary coins like gold, silver and copper but they were coins which were formed from diamond. Being the reason as to why such a glow was put off the moment the light of their flashlights came in contact with them, for Doodlebug there was no reason why she couldn't take a few home. While Doodlebug stuffed a few within her pockets without being seen, she done so while the others were too busy marveling at them.

Being round like a coin, there were some the size of a penny, a quarter and a half dollar. While all of the diamond coins were from a fourth inch thick to half inch, they were all smooth besides three fourths of the center of both sides. For as the center on both sides were cut to form half of a globe, just as the two matched up equally to form one whole. Just as it seemed like all of them were flawless, they were without any stains, chips or cracks.

After Jenna finished looking at the coins she scooped up, she gently put them back from where they came. While making her way around the mound of coins as Breanna followed, she saw this stone edge which ran straight across the center of a wall. Just as it shelved quite a few objects like this short sword and this diamond jeweled scepter, it also shelved these two extravagant crowns. Without touching anything as Jenna looked, Breanna told her those were the belongings of a king and queen, not of a princess or a prince.

Knowing what Breanna told her had to be true, Jenna moved on just as she made a complete sweep of the room. While seeing nothing else besides what she had already seen, she asked Breanna if there possibly could be a hiding spot behind a stone either on the floor or on the wall. With an answer of its possible being heard from Breanna, Jenna told everybody to start checking every stone out. Just as she and her little sister checked the stones along side of the wall, Breanna and Podgy cover the floor.

Just as they made five clean sweeps throughout the room, not a single stone was found loose. With the treasure room being another dead end, it wasn't long till they left from it. While having to go back the way they came, they made it through alright with no complaints. After making it all the way out of the passageway from the treasure room, to the throne room and out to the flight of steps, right down them they went.

Once they made it down they were stuck with the choice of four different passageways to go. While splitting up again into two groups, Doodlebug and Podgy took off to the left just as Jenna and Breanna took off to the right. Just as they told the other which passageway they were going to take before they took off. For as both groups took the passageways that were the closes to the flight of steps. While both passageways had signs that the anguipede had been through them, both passageways also curved like a fourth of a circle.

While both groups were moving the same pace, the moment they came to the passageway ends they saw each other across the other side of this huge empty room which they were led to. Just as the two groups united in the room's center, Breanna told them that it could be one of a few things, a place where the people of Sole gathered to eat; done their trading or it was a shelter for whatever threats they may have had to deal with. With four toppled doors lying on the floors from the beginning of the passages to the end, it made much more since that it was a shelter.

Being a least likely place for a princess to try to hide anything, Jenna told everybody to start searching every stone. While knowing that it was going to take a little time to cover every stone, what Jenna wasn't so sure of was exactly how much time they had to look. With the crown and gem being like a needle and the castle being a haystack, Jenna started to think they were going to be impossible to find. Just as the thought started to slowly pluck away at her mind, it soon became forgotten the moment she came upon this large wobbly stone on the floor.

With excitement filling her hope that was starting to run low up again, Jenna called for everybody to help her. Just as the stone was long as her both ways, the moment everybody got to where she was her little sister blurted out, "Yeah and wouldn't you know it sis, here I thought it was going to be a big stone." After Doodlebug's sarcasm they all wedged their fingers down through an exposed seem on one side and lifted together. Being quite heavy but not as heavy as they thought it was going to be, they soon got it lifted up and flipped over just as cloud dust rolled.

Once they got the stone flipped over it wasn't long until they shined their flashlights down into the darkness. While becoming completely shocked from a disturbing sight, Jenna had a really bad feeling that was where the crown and gem more likely would be found. For as what became seen down in the darkness looked to be a graveyard. Just as there were piles upon piles of human bones lying uncover on the floor of a room that looked to be rather large.

Eerie as the scene looked, the thought of having to venture down and see if the crown and gem was hidden down there was even eerier than one could believe. While knowing that she had to check it out and see, Jenna told them that she would go down and have a look around. Just as she laid her field hockey stick down and stuck her flashlight in her pocket, she soon started down the rope that was after tying an end off around the stone which covered the hole. While descending slowly down, the others shined their flashlights down for her to see.

Just as soon as her feet touched bottom, she pulled out her flashlight and shined it around. While seeing a large squared room, Jenna also saw quite a few holes punctured through the stone walls from tunnels that were behind them. With such a grizzly sight for her eyes having to see, hidden in great slumber were the tears of thousands of woeing sorrows of lost hope. While being a shelter to hide in, it looked more like the people of Sole were rustled up and corralled like a herd of cattle before getting slaughtered by the anguipedes.

After turning completely around and getting a good look at the heart wrenching scene, Jenna put away her flashlight and headed back up the rope. Just as soon as she made it up she told them what she saw. While there after she untied her rope from the stone, wound it up and picked her field hockey stick up. Just as they flipped the stone back over the hole, Jenna told them it was time for them to move on and search elsewhere. Just as they decided to split up again and check out the other two passageways. While leaving out the way they came, the same groups made their way through the last two passageways.

With the passageway Doodlebug and Podgy were in being somewhat short with two flights of steps going down, they ended in the middle of another short passage way which led to a room on each end. While heading right to the room at the end, Podgy pointed up and out in front of him and told Doodlebug, "Look, a cob web." Just as she came to a stop and looked up at it, she replied by saying, "Yeah that's a cob web alright but I don't see the cob that made it anywhere around do you." After hearing that Podgy gave her a weird look and didn't say anything else about it.

Once they made it to the room, they saw a huge mess of what looked to be busted stone jars which once held food. While being a slump-hole of a mess, they turned around and headed back up the passageway to the other room. Just as they were heading up the passageway, Podgy pulled out one of those diamond coins from his pocket and showed it to Doodlebug. Just as he told her that he was going to take it to Kook's Coin Shop and see what it's worth.

Causing Doodlebug to stop, she took the coin from his hand and asked him where Kook's Coin Shop was at, if it was where he came from or where. After telling her that it was there in FallenForHer, on

Bot Boulevard and was ran by a young lady named Colleen Mirel, a thunderous rumble was heard. A thunderous rumble which caused Doodlebug to drop the coin from becoming startled. Just as coin shattered the moment it hit the floor. While giving Doodlebug and Podgy quite a scare, it done the same to Jenna and Breanna who were nearing the end of the passageway they were in.

Just as each of them asked the other what was that, they all answered the others question with a shrug of the shoulders and with the same answer, "Thunder." While after a couple of minutes passed by and no more was heard they didn't make a big deal of it. Just as Doodlebug and Podgy started moving again so did Jenna and Breanna. With the end of the passageway Jenna and Breanna were in was in their sight, they saw a spiraling set of steps leading up. While the passageway that they made their way through having a pile of three anguipede carcasses which had gotten caught in a spear trap from the walls, they knew there were bound to be more traps a head of them lying in their path.

Being obvious where they were being led to was to none other than the princess tower, Jenna and Breanna kept moving towards the spiraling set of steps. Just as they came upon the steps and before they came to a complete stop beneath their feet they felt the stone as it started giving away. While quickly turning and sprinting back as a rumbling sound was heard. The moment they turned back around to have a look, they watched as the steps turned and became a slide for a sled runner. Knowing that it was going to be a challenge to climb up, Jenna was up for the challenge.

After flashing their flashlights along side of the wall that they were able to see of the once known steps and after seeing no holes in the wall, Jenna leaped over the stone that cause the steps to change. Just as she started up the sled running slide, Breanna soon followed. While fighting with the slide as they climbed, both Jenna and Breanna slide back down to the beginning a few times ever before making it halfway up. With the first time being with Jenna just as she lost her grip and started sliding down, she couldn't help it when she plowing right into Breanna who went down with her. Just as the same scenario happened more than once, once after they made it little over half way up and once when they were within three yards of being up. The moment they finally made it up they were relieved.

Relieved as they were after conquering the climb, stunned was what they became seconds afterwards. For as sitting there in the open on a pedestal in the center of the room was none other than the crown and gem. White as a stainless cloud was the jeweled princess crown, white as a pure cloud could possibly be, for as Jenna's and Breanna's reflection from it they could see. Sparkling with its glory as the crown was doing, so was the heart shaped diamond gem sitting so gracefully in the center of it. While with the crown and gem in sight, for Jenna it seemed too good to be true. Just as Breanna had the same feeling as Jenna, she followed her around the room as she look out through each window she passed by and back at the crown and gem.

Once she was a step away from making it halfway around, the moment she took the next step that stone sunk down just as an echoing blunt ka-thoop sound became heard down throughout the slide. Just as Jenna and Breanna made their way back around to see what made the sound, the moment they came upon the slide there along side of the walls sets of four holes scaling down as far as they could see was seen. While knowing what projects from them, Jenna knew that they were going to have to be extremely careful when sliding back down. For as Jenna told Breanna that when they did go down they would have to keep their feet laid flat on their sides and their face so they could slide right underneath all of the lowest holes.

Just as Jenna told Breanna to go ahead and remove her backpack and unzip it, she then turned towards the crown and gem and slowly made her way towards them. After doing like Jenna asked, Breanna followed right along. Once Jenna was a step away from the crown and gem, the moment her foot stepped down on the stone in front of her a crackling sound from up above was heard. While looking up as they shined their flashlights towards the ceiling, they saw long splintering cracks growing wider and wide while the ceiling was starting to bow down.

While crumbling mortar started rain down, Jenna took her eyes off of the ceiling and grabbed the crown and gem from the pedestal and crammed them into the backpack. Just as she zipped the backpack up afterwards, she told Breanna to toss it down the slide and then go down afterwards. While right afterwards she told her she would follow. Doing like Jenna told her to do, Breanna rushed over to the slide, tossed the backpack down it and then slide down herself.

Knowing once she lifts her foot from the stone the entire ceiling was going to fall in, Jenna knew she needed to give Breanna a chance to make it to the bottom and get out from the slide before she headed down. While watching as spears shot out as Breanna started down, Jenna could only pray that she made it down safely. Just as Jenna started counting to ten the moment Breanna was completely out of her sight, she figured that would be plenty of time for her to reach the bottom. While the ceiling kept cracking and mortar kept spewing down, the moment Jenna made it to ten she made tracks to the slide.

Right after her foot come off of the stone just as it sprung back up the entire ceiling fell, while falling right behind it was this large stone boulder. Right at the very moment Jenna started down the slide, the ceiling hit the floor just as the boulder hit the pedestal quaking the entire castle. Just as cloud dust rolled outwards and then straight up, it also rolled down the slide. While Jenna was heading down head first on her belly down the slide while trailing behind her field hockey stick which she tossed down first, the cloud dust was moving faster than her.

From nipping at the soles of her feet to racing toward the nostrils of her nose which would foul up her breathing, Jenna had no idea about the cloud dust which had already engulfed most of her. While keeping her eyes closed as she slid down, all that she was able to hear was the wind whistling pass her ear and the sound of the spears going off inches above her. That was all up until the stone boulder fell over with the pedestal and rolled across the floor before rolling down the slide. For as the moment the boulder started down the slide it bounced rolled, just as it made quite a thunderous sound. While snapping all of the spears which struck it on the way down, it caused a plinking sound.

With everything happening so fast, the rattling of the castle scared Doodlebug and Podgy silly. Just as they were searching throughout the room which was full of baskets, the moment the thunderous sound was heard and the castle shook they flew out of the room. While believing that the castle was falling down, they ran down the passageway and then the other. With their hearts running faster than they were, the moment they came bursting out of the passageway they nearly plowed right into one of the two anguipedes that were searching around. For as the one they bout plowed into was heading for the same passageway they came out of, while the other was heading for the one Jenna and Breanna were in.

Just feet away from plowing into the anguipede, the moment Doodlebug and Podgy saw it and the other they slid as they tried to stop. With eye contacted being made with the one they bout plowed into, Doodlebug knew that it was the one she had previously knocked out. With such a sinister grin looking down at her and Podgy, Doodlebug had a bad feeling that paybacks were going to be hell. Just as Doodlebug's and Podgy's eyes were bugged out when eye contact was made, Doodlebug somehow found a little humor in it for as she flickered off and on a smile. Just as she told the anguipede, "You look like one of those goofball toys that Billbie use to play with." While after telling the anguipede that, it let out a roar.

While their eye contact ended as they tried to turning as they were still sliding, they fell to the floor right at the moment they turned. Being successful as Doodlebug was just as she was able to successfully get right up and move on towards the passageway and away from the anguipede, Podgy wasn't as lucky. For as the moment he made it up, he was lifted on up into the air by the rear of his britches. Just as the anguipede punctured a hole through rear end of his pants with the middle point of his pitchfork right below the beltline.

Once Podgy started yelling it caused Doodlebug to stop and turn back around. After seeing Podgy fifteen plus feet up in the air swinging his arms and legs around, she came rushing back. While coming back with a furry, Doodlebug brought out the artillery just as she let steal ball after steel ball rip from her slingshot. Just as her aim was right on target and having not a ball to miss, all of her effort that she was putting out to save Podgy seemed to be doing no good. With some of the balls hitting the anguipede in the face, on the forehead or at the throat area, Doodlebug also had to contend with the two snake heads of the front which were taking strikes at her.

As the battle to save Podgy from the anguipede ragged on it wasn't long until Jenna came sliding out from the slide. Just as she came sliding out about two and a half yards across the floor while knocking over Breanna who was waiting for her. While the cloud dust rolled right over top of them blinding their vision and causing them to cough, it rolled right on through the passageway. Just as the cloud dust seemed to be unbearable, the sound of the boulder that was heading their way gave them a very good reason to cope with it and get out of the way. For as Jenna quickly got up, located Breanna and helped her up just as she pulled her over along side of the wall and told her to become one with it and what so ever don't move.

Pan caking their selves up against the wall while looking away from the rolling cloud dust and from the oncoming boulder, it wasn't long until the boulder came hurling down the end of the slide. While flying out from it afterwards while missing Jenna and Breanna by a couple of inches, the boulder tunneled through the cloud dust as it kept going on down the passageway. Just as the outer portion of the cloud dust started rolling backwards while the inner followed the boulder and moved forward, a clattery clanking sound trailed behind was heard. For as all of the broken stone spears which the boulder demolished came down the slide were on their way down.

Shortly after the clattery clanking sounds came to a stop, there soon came a plinking sound further back through the passageway where the boulder was heading. While knowing that the boulder just wiped out the spears which the three anguipedes had gotten caught in, what they didn't know was what made the loud, "OOF", sound shortly afterwards. With the sound being a little too loud to be made from a human, Jenna was quick to rule out that it was made by her little sister or by Podgy.

Just as the cloud dust was dying down, it wasn't long afterwards till two beams of light were seen shining across the floor. While realizing that it was their flashlights they soon picked them up right along with the backpack and the field hockey stick which were unharmed. With the settling of the cloud dust thinning throughout the passageway Jenna and Breanna wasted no time to head out of it. For as they had nothing else to do beside find Doodlebug and Podgy and get the heck out of there.

CHAPTER THIRTEEN

Start

THE HIGH WATER OF HELL

Being hoisted over fifteen feet up in the air by the rear end of his pants, Podgy who was scared and became in great fear of his life thought for sure his time was drawing near. While the human part of the anguipede was having fun toying around with him, Doodlebug was doing everything she possibly could to save him. While Doodlebug kept shooting at the anguipede, it wasn't long until she saw this huge boulder come hurling out of the passageway her sister and Breanna went in. Just as soon as the boulder came flying out it plowed into the anguipede that was heading towards that direction. With a loud, "OOF", sound being heard the moment the boulder stuck the anguipede it was contemporaneous with the moment Jenna and Breanna heard an "OOF."

Just as the, "OOF", sound caused the anguipede which had Podgy held up in the air to turn halfway around to where the sound came from, another sound started to be heard. "Rip, Rip, Rip." While the sound of the rear end of Podgy's pants started ripping, it was within a few seconds afterwards till he came falling down from the anguipede's pitchfork. While landing hard the moment he hit the floor just as the wind got knocked out of him, all he could hear while laying flat on his face was, "Podg, get up, I don't know how long I can hold these snakes off." For as Doodlebug was doing her best at keeping the two snake limbs off of him as he laid there a foot or two out in front of them, by keeping their attention focused on her and not him.

After the anguipede saw what had happened to the other anguipede, it turned on around. While being face with two fresh snake limbs of the back of the anguipede, Doodlebug was sure of herself that they would get the better hand and devour Podgy. Just as she started firing at the two snake limbs, they like the front two took strikes at her. After firing off a couple of rounds, Doodlebug watched as the anguipede made his way over towards the one that got struck by the boulder. With it being a perfect opportunity to help Podgy get up, Doodlebug knew that it was a perfect opportunity for her to go around and pick up a few of the steel balls she shot at the anguipede which she was running low on.

While rushing over to Podgy, Doodlebug caught a glimpse of her sister and Breanna heading out of the passageway. Just as she noticed that the anguipede that she was fighting with caught a glimpse of her sister and Breanna while heading for the anguipede that got plastered by the boulder. While yelling look out sis, the anguipede drew back his pitchfork and threw it towards Jenna and Breanna. After hearing her little sister, just the pitchfork went sailing through the air, Jenna and Breanna was able to jump out of the way in the nick of time.

With a blunt vibrating metal sound becoming heard shortly after the pitchfork struck the wall within side of the passageway that Jenna and Breanna came out of, it wasn't long afterwards until they had their hands full with trying to fight off the anguipede. Finding their selves pinned up against a wall outside and away from the passageway, all Jenna was able to do was take swings at the front two snake limbs as they took strikes at her and Breanna who was standing behind her. Just as she kept swinging her field hockey stick back and forth knocking the heads of the snake limbs away, there soon came a break as to where she and Breanna had an opportunity to get away. After knocking one of the snake heads silly, they took off towards where Doodlebug and Podgy where at. While just as soon as they took off running they heard Doodlebug yell as she was pointing back towards them, "Run sis, run, he's right behind you."

Right after hearing that from her little sister just as wind was whooshing by her ears as she was running, Jenna suddenly felt a powerful thump from behind up at shoulder blades causing her to let out a, "Uhhh." While causing her to fall forwards, Jenna soon felt light as a feather just as she was being lifted up into the air. While feeling a set of chompers up against her shoulder blades she knew one of the snake head limbs had her by the back of her shirt. Just as she was being lifted up the entire room soon became a blur just as she was turned in midair.

Once she came to a disoriented stop, all she could see was hideous at its purest form looking down at her with a smile from end to end full of hunger. With teeth showing Jenna knew purée food she was soon to be if she couldn't find it within herself to break free and get away. Just as the anguipede retched down to grab her, he told her, from limb to limb he was going to pull her apart; from limb to limb he was going suck her blood all out and then pull off her head and eat her heart. After hearing that and just as his hands were approaching her, Jenna swung her field hockey stick just as she told him, "I don't think so, hog nose."

While driving the anguipede's hands away from her as she struck them, she does once again as they come her way. Right after driving the anguipede's hands away from her the second time, Jenna heard her little sister holler the craziest thing, "Hang in there sis." While wanting to reply to her little sister, Jenna knew that it would be a bad idea. Just as she drove off the anguipede's hands once more for the third time, she started seeing steel balls hitting the anguipede's face. Just as soon as the steel balls started to be seen striking the anguipede's face, the smell of smoke coming from below she started to inhale.

With a fire being started by Breanna and Podgy from all of what was packed within his backpack including the backpack its self, the moment they had it raging they grabbed a strap each and slung it up towards the belly of the anguipede. Just as the huge ball of fire hit the anguipede right beneath his bellybutton and the top of his kilt causing him to bellow, the blazing backpack fell back down. While burning molten plastic material from the backpack had became smeared on the anguipede just as it was starting to catch his kilt on fire, down from above Jenna fell.

As Jenna came falling down backwards, the anguipede went falling backwards too like a redwood while trying to put out the fire that was burning on him. Just as Doodlebug saw her sister as she started to fall, she cried out, "No sis." As tears were streaming down the sides of Doodlebug's face and trickling off as she watched as her sister came falling down, she was fortunate that Podgy was able to catch her sister. After being thanked and hugged for saving her and being thanked and hugged from Doodlebug for saving her sister, Podgy let Jenna down out of his arms.

Right after Jenna was out of Podgy's arms and was standing on her feet, she told her little sister and Podgy that she and Breanna already found and have the gem and crown of Princess Antoinette and that they needed to leave as soon as possible. After telling them that, Jenna told them, "Come on, let's go", just as she led the way to the castle doors. Just as they came to the doors it took two of them on each side to pull each one open. Once they pulled open the doors, all they could see was a thick wall of white cloud that was until it sunk as it flowed on into the castle.

Just as the cloud wall sunk it unveiled a female anguipede along with two other males' stands behind her out at her sides. While giving quite a startle to Jenna, it also had done the same to the rest as they were bout ready to move forward. While before Jenna knew it, she heard her little sister loudly asked, "Who in the snake world is that hot rocken morocca mamba." After hearing that from her little sister, Jenna told her that it wasn't the time to be silly.

While with a dress made up of tens of thousands rattlers of a rattle snake, it quivered with very slight movement causing it to put off a morocca sound. Just as the dress strapped over the shoulders, it also arched around each snake limb while coming to sharp point down in between each. While with her dress the female anguipede also wore a crown upon her bald head which was made up of hundreds of human jaw bones. While having black dagger like fingernails which could easily decapitate the head from a human; the vicious look of her face could do the very same. With her unique dress and crown, the female anguipede held a very unusual scepter. For as it was made up of eight human spines attached to skulls, four on one end and four on the other end with the spines woven together.

Right after eye contact was made, the female anguipede who was staring straight at Jenna asked, "Going somewhere." While after replying, "Yeah far from here", Jenna heard a holler far from behind back inside of the castle. A holler from the anguipede they just battled, for as he hollered, "Princess Achlys, they killed my brother and they bout killed me." Just as she heard the anguipede tell her that he heard them say they found the gem and crown of Princess Antoinette.

After the aguipede finished, Princess Achlys told him, "Boganose, the loss of your brother Noseboga will be avenged here and now by

133

us on those who killed him." While a little laughter broke out by Doodlebug, she then blurted out, "Anybody with four nostrils would bound to have a nose packed full of bogas." Finding no humor as Princess Achlys stared at Doodlebug, Princess Achlys told her, "I hate the taste of sour blood but Boganose doesn't." After telling her that, Princess Achlys looked straight at Jenna who was standing in front and told her, "You must be the leader and you must be the one who has the gem and crown of Princess Antoinette." Just as she went on and told Jenna to hand them over and her life would be spared.

With trouble in front of them and behind, Jenna asked her little sister if she knows how the shape of a flame goes. While after hearing yeah from her, Jenna told her to follow that path and floor it towards the right with Podgy while she and Breanna goes left and then they'll meet up at the flame's tip. For as Jenna meant they would meet up at the cloud's end. Right after hearing, "Scramble", from her sister, Doodlebug took off towards the right while swerving by the three anguipede's in front of her just as Podgy followed. Just as Jenna took off at the same time to the left with Breanna following, like her little sister and Podgy a path through the cloud was left behind.

While the two male anguipedes were ordered to split up and follow the paths that became made through the cloud, Princess Achlys and Boganose headed straight up the middle in between the two paths. Being quite mobile and made to move very quickly and quietly, it wasn't long until the two male anguipedes were hot on their trails. Just as all four realized that trouble was coming upon them fast, they also noticed that through the cloud they were making a path. While they all had the same idea which was to sink down within side of the cloud and move slow, they done so not to only hide their selves but to stop making a path leading to them.

While concealing their selves within the cloud, what they all forgot was they couldn't conceal the scent of their blood from the blood thirsty blood hounds. Just as they continued moving in the form of a flame without making a visible path through the cloud, it wasn't long until a bump on the behinds of Doodlebug and Podgy were felt. Just as Doodlebug yelled, "Run for it Podg", right afterwards, the two found their selves running in place as they were being lifted up in the air. Once they were lifted up out of the cloud they heard, "Thought you could get away did you." After hearing that just as Doodlebug and Podgy where dangling down from the back of their pants from the mouths of two snake limbs, Doodlebug replied sarcastically back by saying, "How did you ever guess."

Right after Doodlebug replied, the anguipede told her and Podgy that he was going to take them to Princess Achlys. Just as the anguipede started moving, Doodlebug told Podgy not to worry just hang in there. While dangling down by the rear of their pants as they were kept from the sight of the anguipede, Doodlebug had no way to fire her sling shot at him or at any of his snake limbs. Just as she and Podgy stayed quiet while hovering above the cloud as the anguipede was taking them to Princess Achlys, all Doodlebug could hope for was that her sister and Breanna would save them.

Just as the other anguipede male was closing in on Jenna and Breanna, the two were lucky when they came upon this stone wall from the remnants of a house. With the wall being right at six feet tall and eight feet wide, it seemed like an ideal hiding place. While the two became one with the wall as they leaned up against it, they came to finding out that it was rather wobbly. With the condition of the wall being unstable, the two didn't have much of a choice besides staying put and hoping for the best.

Being completely quiet and still, it wasn't long until Jenna and Breanna started to hear movement near the other side of the wall. While the noise grew closer and closer, it soon came to a stop. Just as Jenna and Breanna looked at each other with a wondering look of their faces, they heard an exhale of air from above followed by, "Did you think this wall was going to hide you from me." After hearing that they looked up only to see a sinister grin on an anguipede's face that was looking down at them.

Marked as targets by its glimmering eyes filled full of hunger, Jenna and Breanna were also marked as targets to feed the hunger of Princess Achlys and the others. While with its sinister grin and glimmering eyes, its nostrils heavily shuffled. Just as the anguipede had short white ear length hair, he was bald on top. Bald with a large dark circular mark on his forehead, just above his left eye.

Not being anxious of becoming the anguipede's dinner, Jenna was quick about coming up with a solution to that problem. While looking up at him, she yelled, "Mr. Gorbaboga, tear down this wall", while with all of her strength afterwards she gave the wall a good shove. Just as the wall fell forwards, the anguipede didn't have a chance to move out of the way. While not crushing the anguipede, it fell on top of its front limbs and crushed them just as he screamed out in pain.

Becoming stuck just as its front limbs were wedged underneath the rock wall, right after he screamed out the anguipede swung his pitchfork at Jenna and Breanna. Just as they jumped out of the way, they turned away and took off running. Little after they took off and were more or less ten yards away, a whooshing sound right above their heads was heard. For as the anguipede's pitchfork went flying over their heads.

Right after the pitchfork flew by, it soon struck the ground while a few seconds later Jenna and Breanna passed by it. Shortly after passing by the pitchfork, just as the stuck anguipede was out of their sight they came to a stop. Just as Jenna slowly turned completely around scouting out for any movement, she then looked at Breanna and told her, "We got to find my little sister and Podgy and get out of this place." After seeing no movement anywhere around after having another look, they took off towards this large standing stone building which had a bell tower.

With the stone building being about thirty to forty yards away and being a fourth of the size of the castle, what it looked like was a church. While knowing if they could get up to the bell of the tower their view would be unlimited, they also knew that getting up there might only be wishful thinking. Running like they had wings on their feet like Hermes, it didn't take Jenna and Breanna very long to reach the stone building. Soon after finding the entrance way in, it was exactly what they had expected it to be, a church.

The moment they entered in and saw what it was just as it looked to be untouched by the anguipedes, they made their way by the stone pews. Once they made their way by the pews and then the altar they came across a few scrolls in the pulpit. While unrolling one part way Jenna started reading a verse from Ezekiel, "Now as I beheld the living creatures, behold one wheel upon the earth by the living creatures, with his four faces." After she read that it sent a cold chill down her spine, just as she dropped the scroll and told herself Bug is in trouble.

While looking out towards the pews, there to the right side close to the entranceway Jenna saw a passageway. While knowing that could only be for one thing which was to go up to the bell tower, it didn't take her and Breanna long to head for it. With narrow spiraling steps leading up, the moment they retched top the first thing they saw was the bell. While having a clear view of their surroundings it was what Jenna had hoped for just as it wasn't long until she spotted her little sister. For as her little sister was standing by an anguipede just like Podgy.

Just as Jenna looked on, she saw Princess Achlys and Boganose heading in the direction of where her little sister and Podgy were at with the anguipede. After seeing where her little sister and Podgy were and seeing that they were in trouble, Jenna took off down the bell tower just as Breanna followed. While Jenna and Breanna were on their way to try to save Doodlebug and Podgy, the anguipede was wondering how he was going to save his mind from becoming corrupted from Doodlebug's relentless antics which she was bellowing out. For as the anguipede knew he couldn't go ahead and kill her or let her go on the count he would meet a deadly fate from Princess Achlys.

While the anguipede had already stopped moving just as it let Doodlebug and Podgy down but not loose of the rear end of their pants, it kept telling Doodlebug to be quiet. With the relentless questioning about bogas and about his nose, the anguipede wasn't sure how much more he could take. With the antics becoming more annoying than ever before, the annoyance only grew a whole lot worse. Especially when the anguipede let off a rumbling flabby sound which was full of air and gas, which penetrated down through the cloud beneath him while clearing away a huge circular patch away from around him.

With laughter breaking loose between Doodlebug and Podgy, over a million things came flying out of Doodlebug's mouth as it started running over a hundred miles an hour. From, "Boy you're lucky you weren't standing over a fire because you would have blasted to outer space like a rocket ship." To, "Boy if you got a nose full of bogas, you're lucky you don't have to smell what we have to smell." With every thinkable thing in between being blurted as she laughed, her laughter like Podgy's soon blinded both of them. Just as the anguipede started letting more and more rumbling flabby sound off which were full of air and gas, he let go of them from not knowing what was happening to him.

After being released, Doodlebug and Podgy fell through the cloud and down to the ground while laughing. While becoming literally senseless from not knowing they had a chance to get away, all they done was rolled around on the ground while holding their stomachs as they laughed. Just as the anguipede was more concern about what was happening to him, he completely forgot all about them. Just as he tossed down his pitchfork and started turning around in circles while looking down. With a confused state of mind, the anguipede didn't even notice Jenna and Breanna when they snuck in.

Once Jenna and Breanna located Doodlebug and Podgy by their un-concealable laughter which could be heard coming from down within the cloud, they quickly got both of them up. While right after they had Doodlebug and Podgy up from the ground, the anguipede let off another rumble which caused Doodlebug to let out a, "Blaaa, ha, ha, haaa, ha, ha, haaa", and fall back down in a sea of her laughter. Just as soon as they got Doodlebug back up, they managed to take off. Just as they were heading for the cloud's edge, it wasn't easy for Doodlebug and Podgy to stop laughing for as their laughter followed.

The moment they came upon the cloud's edge and Jenna was ready to break the water of the cloud to from the steps back down, from behind came a whishing sound, like the sound of beads rolling quickly around the inside of a morocca. While right afterwards the whishing sound turned right into a rattling sound which followed by none other than the voice of Princess Achlys. Just as she said, "Planning on jumping to your deaths, because the fall is a long one." After hearing that, Jenna, Doodlebug, Breanna and Podgy quickly turned around. Just as they saw Princess Achlys who had a smirk on her face and Boganose who had his pitchfork drawled back ready to make shich ka bobs out of them.

Giving a response to Princess Achlys question, Jenna told her, "Yeah if it means getting away from the two of you." Just as she went on and added, "Because falling to our deaths would be more pleasant than becoming snake food." After hearing that Princess Achlys laughed a little before telling her to hand over the crown of clouds and the gem. While right afterwards she told Jenna if she didn't, then before her very eyes each one that is with her will be torn from limb to limb.

While having a wondering thought of why she wanted the crown of clouds and gem of Princess Antoinette for, Jenna simply asked Princess Achlys. While with her question there came an answer. Just as Princess Achlys told Jenna, "The crown of clouds and the gem of Princess Antoinette was a symbol of superiority over the anguipedes years ago and after the fall of the Kingdom of Sole and until the two are destroyed they'll always be. Right after answering Jenna's question, Princess Achlys told her to hand the two over because no humans will ever rule here again.

Without saying anything or taking her eyes off of Princess Achlys, Jenna told her little sister to load up and get ready. Just as she removed the coil of rope from her shoulder and handed it to Podgy, she told him to loop up a lasso for her. While right afterwards she told Breanna to stay behind them. With her field hockey stick held tightly in her hands, Jenna was ready for a fight.

With a stare down between Jenna and Princess Achlys holding strong, Jenna soon told her little sister to aim for Boganose's nose and fire. While right afterwards she told Podgy to toss the lasso over one of snake heads of Princess Achlys and pull back as hard as he possibly could. With everything happing so fast and pretty well simultaneously, just as Doodlebug fired and Podgy tossed the lasso, there came Boganose's pitchfork flying. Just as Doodlebug scored a hit on Boganose's upper nose and in between his eyes and Podgy lassoed one of Princess Achlys's limbs and jerked back, right in between Jenna and Doodlebug at shoulder height Boganose's pitchfork flew. Just as the sisters turned and hobbled backwards as it flew by.

Just as Boganose's pitchfork went flying off of the cloud, up went his hands flying to his face. And while the sisters hobbled backwards, Doodlebug fell through the cloud and onto the ground on her rear end, while Jenna bumped into Podgy causing him to let go of the rope and fall through the cloud and to the ground. Just as Jenna's right foot plunged down into the rest of the coiled rope which was lying on the ground, it quickly got tangled up. While before Jenna even knew it, the lassoed limb of Princess Achlys jerked back causing her feet to get pulled out from underneath her.

While her feet got lifted up into the air, her upper body came crashing down through the cloud and onto the ground. Just as her right foot became more tingled, Jenna knew one thing, she was in trouble. And trouble she was in when she found herself sliding feet first forwards on her back. Just as she knew that she was about to become acquainted with Princess Achlys.

While standing defenseless and all alone with Princess Achlys and Boganose, Breanna didn't seem to have much to worry about for the time being. For as Princess Achlys was more concerned with getting the lasso removed from her limb, while Boganose was trying to cope with the two shots he received at his upper nose and in between his eyes. While not having to stand alone for very long as Breanna had to do, it wasn't long until Doodlebug emerged up from the cloud, just as Podgy followed seconds afterwards.

Shorty after Doodlebug and Podgy were standing once again, they all soon saw Jenna get lifted up from the cloud feet first by the lassoed limb of Princess Achlys. Just as Jenna was daggling down by her right ankle from the lassoed limb of the snake's mouth, she soon was hoisted on up into the air. After Princess Achlys retched down and grabbed the rope with her left hand from the snake's mouth of her limb, she lifted Jenna up to eyes view. Being upside down and having up close eye contact with Princess Achlys, Jenna done the only thing knew to do. For as she drove her field hockey stick as hard as she possible could right at the nose of Princess Achlys.

Right after Jenna plastered Princess Achlys nose, Princess Achlys let out a hellacious scream. While Princess Achlys turned sideways quickly just as Jenna swung back with the motion, before Jenna knew it she came swinging forward as Princess Achlys turned back very fast. With Princess Achlys's momentum she let go of the rope and let Jenna go flying through the air. Just as Jenna went flying like a torpedo head first through the air, the rope went right along for the ride while snaking through the air from her right foot. Being a lurid scene for not only Doodlebug to have to see, it was quite horrifying for Breanna and Podgy as well.

With the event happening very fast, nobody had a thought of a chance of trying to prevent it from happening. Just as Jenna went flying through the air she went flying right off of the cloud. Just as Doodlebug dropped her slingshot while letting out an outcry, Breanna and Podgy had to quickly get a hold of her so she wouldn't go plunging off. Just as Doodlebug broke down and fell on her knees and hands in tears, the rope came down and sliced through the cloud.

Less than a second after the rope sliced through the cloud it came to a hard stop. Just as Princess Achlys got her limbs pulled out from underneath of her causing her to fall over backwards, "Ba-whoosh", the air from her fall cleared a huge area off just as the cloud went rolling out from around her, Boganose and even Doodlebug and friends. Just as the lasso around her one limb also noosed up tight the moment it happened. With a hectic scene being seen on both sides the anguipedes and Doodlebug and friends, it also was rather hectic down below the cloud also. For as Jenna was hanging upside down by the tangled rope around her right foot several feet beneath the cloud.

While noticing that Her Lake was still below, Jenna knew even with it there she'd plummet to her death if she were to fall. With a view of Her Lake, Jenna could also see the lit up streets of Her, FallenForHer and Dé Blur. With street lights glowing, car head lights and house lights also could be seen. Just as Jenna was looking down as the rope was turning her around, she knew that she needed to somehow get a hold of the rope and climb back up.

With the night being hectic for those wondering amongst the cloud, the night was quite wondrous for one down below who meows While sitting on a stand looking out the living room window towards the cloud looming in front of the blood moon, was none other than Boom-box Boob. Just as it looked like as if it could see what was going on, the look which could be seen on its face had the look of something was wrong. Just as it looked on, it stood up on its hind legs like a groundhog and started working its arms up and down out in front of it.

Just as Boom-box Boob continued on, from out of nowhere came Sal' Amanda. While after flurrying up from behind Boom-box Boob, she told it that there was no need to worry, because they'll be back soon. Just as Boob-box Boob dropped back down, Sal' Amanda started petting it. While the two continued looking out the window, Sal' Amanda knew that there was a possible chance they wouldn't.

Just as Jenna's mind was going into overdrive from trying to figure a way out of her predicament, it wasn't long until a solution to her problem hit her. While being fortunate enough that she didn't become separated from her field hockey stick, it helped her out of the situation which she was in. Just as she retched the end of her field hockey stick up to the rope and hooked it, she managed walk her hands up the staff of it while getting herself pulled up to the rope. Once she got herself pulled up, she looked straight up towards the long climb which was now facing her.

Being knotless and quite a ways to go, Jenna knew it was going to be a challenging climb. Just as she bit down on the staff of her field hockey stick there in the middle, she wasted no time to start climbing. With the rope drawling moisture, Jenna slide right back down from where she started after making it little over halfway up. With the slide back down giving her hands quite a burn, it only made Jenna that much more determined to conquer the climb.

Unlike Jenna who was unwilling to give up, Doodlebug who thought she had lost her sister simply gave up. Just as she sat on her knees hunched over on the ground crying which was cloud covered once again, Breanna and Podgy stood in front of her waiting for the Boganose to strike. While Breanna had a club in her hands that she found lying on the ground, Podgy had a rock in each of his hands. For as the two were bellicose.

Being ready for a fight, it wasn't long until Boganose rushed forwards at them. Just as Breanna struck the side of one of the heads of the snake with her club, Podgy threw one rock into the other's mouth while driving the other stone he had down on top of its head. While causing Boganose to quickly move backwards, it also caused him to run into Princess Achlys who was lying on the ground unseen beneath the cloud. Just as it caused him to go falling over backwards, over top of Princess Achlys and on down to the ground.

After Boganose crashed to the ground, just as the cloud rolled out and around as it cleared out, Breanna and Podgy watched as Princess Achlys sit up and pull one of the skull spines from her scepter. While right after they watched as she ran the spine end across the lasso which was noosed around her limb. Just as the rope split halfway into, here came the cloud rolling back covering up the ground. With only the upper body of Princess Achlys being seen, it wasn't long until up from the ground she came as she became freed. Just as the sound of the rope zipping across the ground was heard before falling off of the cloud.

Just as Podgy had a chance to round up a couple more rocks, he like Breanna was ready for Princess Achlys. Shortly after Princess Achlys became freed and was standing once again, she wasted no time in heading Breanna's and Podgy's way. With the spine skull in her left hand and the rest of her scepter in her right hand, she knew it was a matter of time till feasting time. Just as she was making her way closer and closer to Breanna and Podgy, Boganose rose up from the cloud and stood up.

While Princess Achlys was coming closer, Breanna and Podgy watched as she drew back her left arm. Just as Princess Achlys was holding onto the skull with the spine pointing out, she gave Podgy a cold stare right before swinging her arm forward and letting the spine skull fly. Just as the spine skull was heading straight for him, up out of the cloud a couple of feet in front of him came a field hockey stick slicing up through followed by Jenna who then emerged. Just as she swung her field hockey stick breaking the oncoming spine skull in half.

After scaring Podgy half silly from bursting up through the cloud in front of him and breaking the oncoming spine skull in half, Jenna looked straight at Princess Achlys and told her, "You thought I fell to my death didn't you." With a mean look on her face like never seen before, Princess Achlys replied by telling Jenna, "You're going to wish you had." Just as she pulled another spine skull from the other end of her scepter she drew back her arm. While just as she was about to let the spine skull go flying at Jenna, a voice was heard, "Sis is still alive, what, sis is still alive, WHAT."

Right afterwards, leaping up from the cloud came a joyful Doodlebug. Just as Jenna, Breanna and Podgy turned around; here came Doodlebug rushing forwards just as she tackled her sister to the ground. While Princess Achlys launched the spine skull seconds after Jenna turned around, it flew inches away from Doodlebug's neck after tackling her sister and as they started falling to the ground. Just as Doodlebug was telling her sister how much she loved her and how much she meant to her, Breanna and Podgy went another round with Boganose after rushing forwards.

With a heated battle ragging on, Jenna told her little sister, "Let's kick some snake butt and get out of here." With a reply of, "I'm with you on that sis", they both sprung up from the cloud only to see a spine skull heading straight at Breanna. Before Jenna had a chance to move and try to knock it away, Breanna swung her club at it only to have it pierce through the other side. While half of the spine was sticking out the other side of Breanna's club, she tossed it to the ground.

Just as Princess Achlys was on the verge of pulling another spine skull from her scepter, Doodlebug loaded up her slingshot, pulled back and aimed for her nose and fired. With a hit at her upper and lower nose, it caused Princess Achlys to drop her scepter. While her hands flew up to her face, Jenna told her little sister to do the same to Boganose while she breaks the water from the cloud. Doing like her sister asked just as Boganose was heading their way, Doodlebug loaded up, aimed for his nose and fired just as Podgy threw two more stones at the heads of its front limbs.

Having both of the anguipedes distracted by the punishment they received, Jenna turned away from the snake crowd and swung her field hockey stick down through the cloud. While telling the water of the cloud to break as she swung, water started falling downwards while steps started to form. While telling Breanna to start down them first, Jenna then told Podgy to start down afterwards just as she told both of them whatever they do don't look back. Once Breanna started down and Podgy followed just as the rear end of his pants could be seen opening and closing, 'boof, boof, boof, boof', Jenna told her little sister to go head and start down and she would follow.

Doing like her sister asked, Doodlebug wasted no time on heading down. Right after Doodlebug started down Jenna soon followed. Just as the steps spiraled down to Her Lake, they were blood red like the moon which reflected down onto them. Once Jenna was about six or seven yards down, down from the cloud above came a spine skull just as it flew over her head and struck the step right behind her little sister.

Causing a splashing sound the moment it struck the step just as water splashed up and all around and even down right after it came plunging out from underneath, it gave Doodlebug a reason to stop and turn around. Just as soon as she got turned around she like her sister who was looking back saw Princess Achlys throw another spine skull. Just as it came sailing towards Jenna, she batted it off with her field hockey stick just as it went falling down through the night sky.

Right after Jenna batted the spine skull away, she watched as Boganose who had a huge oblong stone toss it down towards the steps. Just as the stone was four to five feet long, it was right at two feet in width around each of its four sides. The moment that the stone struck the steps, there came a huge splash up and around and down as it fell though. Just as the shattered water came raining down like fire through the night sky so did the steps. Starting from where the stone struck going both ways up and down.

With the scene looking like fire falling down from Heaven, it was what one could call the high water of hell. Just as the steps started to fall and rain down through the night sky, Jenna quickly turned around and floored it down the steps as fast as she could. Just as Jenna turned around and took off down the steps so did her little sister who saw what happened and what was happening. While Breanna and Podgy were much further down nearing the step's end, up where Jenna was at the steps behind her which were shattering were heading closer and closer to her.

After the stone Boganose threw went crashing down through the steps it wasn't long until it fell by Podgy and then Breanna while causing a horrendous splash shortly afterwards when it collided with Her Lake. Right after the stone dropped by them, both of them stopped, turned around and looked up. While seeing what looked to be a rain of fire pouring down from the night sky above, Breanna and Podgy saw the steps shattering right behind Jenna. Just they watched on they saw the steps as they shattered beneath her feet just as she went free falling.

While Jenna fell with the shattered water beneath her feet just as she still was running from instinct, it didn't take long for her to go flying down by her little sister. Just as shattered water followed her down, within five seconds after flying down by her little sister, the step beneath her little sister shattered just as she fell. The moment Doodlebug fell, Jenna flew down by Podgy and then Breanna before crashing into Her Lake. With Jenna's fall being right at two hundred and fifty feet she survived it just like her little sister who came crashing down close by her.

Just as the steps continued shattering, Breanna and Podgy turned back around and took off running on down them. While being so close to the end, they were sure they could make it all the way down and back on solid ground before the rest shattered. While Breanna was able to make it the rest of the way down and to solid ground, Podgy lucked out by twenty or so steps just as he took a short fall down into the lake about eight yards out from shore. Just as he fell down into the lake, out from it came Jenna and her little sister.

Being soaked from head to toe, Jenna and her little sister's hands were prune like just as they were white as snow. While shivering as they were coming out of the lake, the sisters had a smile on their faces. Knowing that they accomplished a great task that was laid before them, it made them feel good about their selves. Once they made it to shore where Breanna was waiting for them at, they looked on and watched as Podgy made his way to shore.

Once Podgy made it out of the water and Jenna made sure everybody was alright, she then asked Breanna for the backpack. After Breanna removed the backpack from her shoulders, she held it out for Jenna to take. While not taking it from Breanna's hands, Jenna simply unzipped it. Just as she removed the Book of Hearts, with much excitement in her calm cool voice she told them, "This is it."

As everybody watched as the Book of Hearts laid in the palm of Jenna's left hand, they watched on as she then removed the crown of clouds of Princess Antoinette from the backpack. While laying it on top of the Book of Hearts afterwards, Jenna then removed the diamond heart shaped gem from the backpack. Just as soon as she pulled out the gem from the backpack, she then laid it on the Book of Hearts there in the center of the crown. Just as the crown and gem melted down within the Book of Hearts, a portion of the cover vanished like the pages about Princess Antoinette.

While everybody watched as the Book of Hearts became a little thinner, Jenna looked towards Breanna just as watched as a portion of her hair vanished. For as one thirteenth of it vanished right before her very eyes. Just as the white hair was gone from Breanna's head, it wasn't that noticeable on the count of her having a thick scalp of hair left. While not saying anything besides smiling instead, Jenna who hid her frown told all of them, "Come on let's go home and get some rest."

CHARACTER INDEX

The Aitch Sisters

1. Jenna Aitch
2. Doodlebug

The Aitch Sister's Friends

1. Baby Doll Stump
2. Breanna "Manikin Ann"
3. Cinerin N' Anna 'O
4. Heather Sówhich
5. Marrian N' Anna 'O
6. Mrs. Shanty
7. Pete Stump
8. Podgy Littlewhich
9. Roorin Tezory, "Rutabaga"

The Thirteen Hearts

1. Makenzie Drells "Kenzie"
2. Sarah Breils
3. Aairrha Breils
4. Baby Doll Stump
5. Susan Sue Sousashoe
6. Okie Ka' Bokie
7. Seven Hairs
8. Samantha Buckles
9. Regina Sumac
10. Amy Poors
11. Mirrha Feeart
12. Monique Tüshoe
13. Gina Aitch

Hell's Hooligans

1. Delusional Dorothy
2. Dizzy Dead Daisy
3. Medusa
4. Metamorphous Corry
5. Xy

The Green Flies

1. Darrin Marsh
2. Andrew David
3. Mickael Alexandra
4. Nick Gwil

Old Field Hockey Opponents

1. Marie W. Marry
2. Sophie Sofasock

FallenForHer Bullpen Wrestler

1. Thule Greenland's Giant, Topper

Characters of the story read in the Book of Hearts by Jenna Aitch

1. Anguipedes
2. Princess Antoinette
3. Prince Lowell
4. Prince Saul
5. The Stranger

Characters from a story in the Book of Hearts read by the Thirteenth Heart, Gina Aitch

1. Three headed panther
2. Princess Athena
3. Living Skeletons

Other Characters

1. Barb Boon
2. Billbie Zilery
3. Boganose
4. Boom-box Boob
5. Burl
6. Colleen Mirel
7. Fiends
8. Jill Aitch
9. Joseph Aitch
10. Limby Leen
11. Noseboga
12. Princess Achlys
13. Princess Miranda
14. Ra-ra Rob
15. Sal' Amanda
16. Salamander Sam
17. Talky
18. The Devil
19. The Faceless Witch of Hades
20. Walky
21. Willard Wilson Drells

CHARACTER DICTIONARY

1. **Aairrha Breils:** (A twenty-two year old young lady, with long dirty blond hair and deep sea blue eyes, who stands five foot five; a young lady from What County; a young lady who played on the field hockey team for the What County question marks as number forty three and as a forward left wing during her high school years, "What?"; a young lady who has the smarts in martial arts; a young lady who is the third member of the Thirteen Hearts; a young lady who is a half sister to Sarah Breils)

2. **Amy Poors:** (A twenty-three and a half year old young lady, with shoulder length black hair and with hazel eyes who stands five foot three; a young lady from Foot County, from the suburb of Dé Blur; a young lady who has a master's degree in chemistry; a young lady who has a wondrous working mind that thinks; a young lady who is the tenth member of the Thirteen Hearts)

3. **Andrew David:** (A twenty seven year old man with blond mushroom cut hair; a man who stands five foot seven and has grayish blue eyes; a man who's skin pigment was tampered with to cause him to change to the color of sewage metallic green; a man who smells like a rotting carcass on the count of the chemical putrescine that's within his body was dabbled with; a man who is the second Greenfly of the Gangrene Gang; also known as D.A.M.N Green Flies)

4. **Anguipedes:** (Unruly mythological creatures; creatures half man and half serpent; creatures with four serpent headed limbs with an upper body of a human; creatures twenty foot long when stretched out, twelve to sixteen foot when moving about; creatures which lived in the center of the cloud that the kingdom of Sole sat on; blood thirsting creatures; creatures that fought with large three pointed pitchforks; creatures read about in the Book of Hearts)

5. **Baby Doll Stump:** (A twenty-four and a half year old young lady, with long straight strawberry red hair and with hazel eyes; a young lady with a face wrecked with freckles and who stands five foot four; A young lady who was without dimples; a jocund young lady; a exuberant young lady, "joie de vivre"; a young lady from Foot County, from the suburb of Dé Blur; a young lady who was the head cheerleader for Dé Blur High during her high school years; a very charitable and caring young lady; a young lady who is the forth heart of the Thirteen Hearts; a older sister to Pete; a long time friend of the Aitch sisters)

6. **Barb Boon:** (A sixty-two year old lady, with short dark brown hair and hazel eyes who stands five foot four; a lady from Foot County, from FallenForHer; a lady who is the town's mayor of FallenForHer and the three surrounding suburbs)

7. **Billbie Zilery:** (An eight year old male child who had dark brownish black frilly curly hair, right along with full of life big brown eyes; an eight year old who passed away from an unknown and incurable disease; a male child who lived in Foot County, from the poverty stricken neighborhood of Grimm Street in FallenForHer; a childhood friend of the Aitch sisters, who was more like a brother to them)

8. **Boganose:** (An unruly mythological creature; a creature half man and half serpent; a creature with four serpent headed limbs with an upper body of a human; a creature twenty foot long when stretched out, twelve to sixteen foot when moving about; a creature which lives in the center of the cloud that the kingdom of Sole once sat on; a blood thirsting creature; a creature that fights with large three pointed pitchforks; a warrior of Princess Achlys; a anguipede who has long yellowish white hair and who is the brother to Noseboga; the anguipede who Jenna first encounters)

9. **Boom-box Boob:** (A three year old fixed female tabby cat; a tabby cat that didn't learn to purr; a tabby cat that was fixed with a harness on its right side which held a small radio; a tabby cat that grew to wearing a small derby hat; a tabby cat that would stand up like a groundhog and work its arms up

and down whenever it tries to get somebody's attention; a tabby cat that belonged to both Jenna and Doodlebug)

10. **Breanna:** (A wondering spirit that escaped from the Book of Hearts and hid in the lock of princess hair which sealed it; a wondering spirit that brought a manikin to life after the lock of hair came in contact with the manikin's head; a wondering spirit of a younger sister of a princess named Miranda; a friend of the Aitch sisters and of Podgy; Breanna aka Manikin Ann)

11. **Burl:** (A twenty-two year old male, with short black hair and eyes of hazel; a male who stands five foot three and is afraid of his own shadow; A witless man whose wits had already out witted his self; a man who lives in Foot County, from the suburb of Fallen; a man who is in love with Seven Hairs; a man who has taken residents at Makenzie Drells house)

12. **Cinerin N' Anna 'O:** (A twenty four year old young lady who has long red black pepper flake hair; a young lady who's hair is in dreadlocks and beaded colorfully up; a young lady who stands five foot four and has hazel eyes; a young lady whose father is Asian and mother is Caucasian; a young lady who was born and raised in Jamaica and is a Jamaican; a young lady plays a electric bass guitar and is rarely seen without her stained-glass sunglasses on; a young lady who is goofy as one can be; a young lady who is in a band called the Gorilla Girl and the Jamaicans; a young lady who is the lead bass guitarist in the Gorilla Girl and the Jamaicans; a young lady who now lives in Foot County, from a apartment on Bot Boulevard in FallenForHer; a young lady who is a cousin of Marrian N' Anna 'O; a young lady who lives with her cousin)

13. **Colleen Mirel:** (A twenty-five year old young lady who has thick long sarsaparilla color hair and spring morning sky blue eyes; a young lady who stands five foot four and has a flicker of a paintbrush flick of freckles; a young lady who is softly spoken; a lady who recently moved to FallenForHer after finishing her duties as a corporal in the Marin Cor; a young lady who opened up a coin shop on Bot Boulevard called Kook's Coin Shop; a mysterious young lady who literally could see right through you)

14. **Darrin Marsh:** (A twenty eight year old man, with short dirty blond hair; a man who stands five foot eight and has blue eyes; a man who's skin pigment was tampered with to cause him to change to the color of sewage metallic green; a man who smells like a rotting carcass on the count of the chemical putrescine that's within his body was dabbled with; a man who is the leader of the Gangrene Gang; also known as D.A.M.N Green Flies)

15. **Delusional Dorothy:** (A twenty-two year old young lady, with dark blue, red and black hair, long and short hair cone spiked out around the bald spots of her shaved head; a young lady with dark blue, red and black splotches of paint on her face; a young lady who stands five foot six and dresses gothic; a young lady who is the singer for Hell's Hooligans the band she's in; a young lady who lives on the road she and her band travels on)

16. **Dizzy Dead Daisy:** (A nineteen your old young lady, with long black beaded dreadlock hair; a young who paints her face like a black and white hypnotic swirl; a young lady who stands five foot five and dresses gothic; a young lady who is the lead bass guitar player for Hell's Hooligans the band she's in; a young lady who's from Acapulco; a young lady who now lives on the road she and her band travels on)

17. **Doodlebug:** (A twenty-one year old young lady, with long wavy luscious pumpernickel color hair; a young lady who stands five foot three and has bluish-green eyes like dioptase; a young lady with a face like a porcelain angel that's so fragile and with dented in dimples; a young lady with a mellifluous voice; a jocund young lady; a exuberant young lady, "joie de vivre"; a young lady who was born with half of a left leg and was equipped with a wheel; a young lady whose curiosity can get her in more trouble than she can get out of; a young lady who loves fishing, painting and wrestling; a young lady who was raised in the poverty stricken neighborhood of Grimm Street; a young lady who played for FallenForHer's East High Orange Bills field hockey team for one season as number thirteen and as a sweeper; a young lady who lives in Foot County, from the suburb of Her at 76th Orange Street; a young lady whose the younger sister of Jenna)

18. **Feinds:** (A being with yellow eyes and charcoal color skin; a being that stands from a foot to a foot and a half tall; a being with cat like toenails and claws; a being with shearing teeth; a being found in hell)

19. **Gina Aitch:** (A twenty-five year old young lady, with long black hair and emerald green eyes; a young lady who stands four foot nine; a jocund young lady; a exuberant young lady, "joie de vivre"; a young lady who is polyglot; a young lady who was put up for adoption the day she was born; a young lady who was adopted by the Lemons from Hope County a hundred and twelve miles away; a young lady who grew up without knowing how to be deceitful or to tell a lie; a young lady who was home taught and rarely got to play with any children her age; a respectful young lady who had a lonely childhood life; a young lady who's a chaser of rainbows; a young lady who after leaving home cross paths with Makenzie and became best friends; a young lady who got to play for the Mimes during Makenzie's final year of high school as number twenty nine and as a goalie; a young lady who is the thirteenth Heart of the Thirteen Hearts; a young lady who is a long lost sister of the Aitch sisters and a identical twin of Jenna)

20. **Heather Sówhich:** (A twenty-one year old young lady with black hair; a young lady who stands five foot three and has ice-blue Eskimo eyes; a young lady who was born and raised in an igloo up in the frigid north in Alaska; a young lady who moved to FallenForHer before her first high school year; a young lady who became best friend during high school; a young lady who got teased allot during her high school years; a young lady who is now studying limnology and volcanology)

21. **Jenna Aitch:** (A twenty-five year old young lady, with long black hair and emerald green eyes; a young lady who stands four foot nine; a jocund young lady; a exuberant young lady, "joie de vivre"; a charismatic young lady; a young lady who has a face of a divided angel, one divided between Heaven and Hell; a young lady who is able to take the good with the bad; a young lady who played for FallenForHer's East High Orange Bills field hockey team as number nine and as a forward left wing; a young lady who was one of the state's top five

field hockey players; a young lady who lives in Foot County, from the suburb of Her at 76th Orange Street; a young lady whose the older sister of Doodlebug; a young lady whose the identical twin of Gina Aitch; a young lady who is determined to save the souls of each of the thirteen princesses)

22. **Jill Aitch:** (A thirty-six year old lady who had long black hair and stood five foot two; a lady who had emerald green eyes; a lady who loved fishing and painting; a lady who was the mother of Jenna, Gina and Doodlebug but never raised Gina; a lady who lived in the poverty stricken neighborhood of Grimm Street; a lady who was married to Joseph Aitch; a lady who passed away from cancer days after Jenna graduated from high school)

23. **Joseph Aitch:** (A thirty-eight year old man who had short black hair and stood six foot three; a man who had sapphire blue eyes; a man who was the father of Jenna, Gina and Doodlebug but never raised Gina; a man who lived in the poverty stricken neighborhood of Grimm Street; a man who was married to Jill Aitch; a man who wrestled for FallenForHer's Bullpen Wrestling organization; a man who went by, The Masked Piñata as his wrestling character; a man who never lost a steal cage match; a man who collapsed in the ring moments before a title match and died in front of Jenna and Doodlebug; a man who's heart gave up on him two weeks after the loss of his wife)

24. **Limby Leen:** (A two and a half foot tall limb that had fallen from a tree; a limb that had two arms and legs and was brought to life by a little girl's imagination; a limb that captivated the imagination of the little girl and the adventures they went on; a limb who had a magical limousine; a limb that turned everyday problems around; a limb that was the best friend of Doodlebug's as a child)

25. **Living Skeletons:** (Skeletons told about to Jenna and Doodlebug by Baby Doll Stump; skeletons, Baby Doll referred to as bones; skeletons which Baby Doll had to help fight off while helping Makenzie Drells to find the crown and emerald heart shaped gem of Princess Athena which the Thirteenth Heart Gina Aitch read about in the Book of Hearts)

26. **Makenzie Drells:** (A twenty-five year old young lady, with long wavy luscious pumpernickel color hair and dioptase color eyes; a young lady who stands five foot five; a young lady who to the Aitch sisters has a ornery pterodactyl smile especially when she was up to no good; a young lady with a mellifluous voice; a young lady who is polyglot; a ravishing young lady; a young lady who is a amateur magician; a young lady who lives in Foot County, from the suburb of Fallen; a young lady who played for the Dé Blur Mimes during her high school years as number thirteen and as a forward right wing; a young lady who never let the Mimes lose a single game during her high school years; a young lady who led the Mimes to a state champion for four straight years; a young lady who formed and leads the Thirteen Hearts; a young lady who is the last of the Drells; a young lady who inherited the Drells estate shortly after her mother, father and little brother's lives were taken away from them in a car accident; a young lady who's heart completely darkened after the loss of her parents and little brother; a young lady who also inherited the Book of Hearts)

27. **Marie W. Marry:** (A twenty-four and a half year old young lady with long curly strawberry red hair and with hazel eyes; a young lady with a face wrecked with freckles and who stands five foot four; A young lady who had deep detent in dimples; a young lady who is persnickety; a young lady who lives in Greenground County; a young lady who played for the Greenground County Gators field hockey team during her high school years as number twenty one and as a forward right wing; a young lady who was next at being the best field hockey play to Makenzie; a young lady who's fighting a losing battle to a disease that was rapidly consuming her life)

28. **Marrian N' Anna 'O:** (A twenty-four year old young lady with long thick soft orange hair; a young lady with hazel eyes and stands five foot four; a young lady with a gorgeous hippo grin; a young lady who played for the Country County Clodhoppers field hockey team during her high school years as number eighteen and as goalie; a young lady who is known by Gorilla Girl; a young lady who is a amateur guitarist; a young lady who is in a band called the Gorilla Girl and the

Jamaicans; a young lady who is the lead guitarist and lead singer for Gorilla Girl and the Jamaicans; a young lady who is a cousin of Cinerin N' Anna 'O; a young lady who now lives in Foot County, from a apartment on Bot Boulevard in FallenForHer; a young lady who is a long time friend of the Aitch sisters)

29. **Medusa:** (A twenty one year old young lady with long braided dirty blond hair; a young lady with her head shaved bald around each of the braids; a young lady who has small white skull with flickering red eyes at the ends of each braid; a young lady who paints her face green and trimmed in black; a young lady who stands five foot five and dresses gothic; a young lady who is the lead electric guitar player for Hell's Hooligans the band she's in; a young lady who lives on the road she and her band travels on)

30. **Metamorphous Corry:** (A twenty two year old young lady with a afro; a young lady who's afro is sculpted to look like several skulls; a young lady who's afro is white and black to bring out the skulls; a young lady who paints her face white like a skull; a young lady who stands five foot five and dresses gothic; a young lady who is the drummer for Hell's Hooligans the band she's in; a young lady who is African American; a young lady who lives on the road she and her band travels on)

31. **Mickael Alexandra:** (A twenty seven and a half year old man with a buzz cut; a man who stands five foot and eight and a half inches and has blue eyes; a man who's skin pigment was tampered with to cause him to change to the color of sewage metallic green; a man who smells like a rotting carcass on the count of the chemical putrescine that's within his body was dabbled with; a man who is the third Greenfly of the Gangrene Gang and who is the nosiest one of them all; also known as D.A.M.N Green Flies)

32. **Mirrha Feeart:** (A twenty five year old young lady who has short blond hair and grayish blue eyes; a young lady who stands five foot two and who's smile never dyes; a young lady who has a nickname Mirror-Mirror; a young lady who lives in Foot County, from the suburb of Dé Blur; a young lady who played for the Dé Blur Mimes during her high school years as

number two and the right midfielder; a young lady who's the photographer of the FallenForHer News Paper; a young lady who is the eleventh Heart of the Thirteen Hearts; a young lady who is a childhood friend of Makenzie)

33. **Monique Tüshoe:** (A twenty four year old young lady with shoulder length black hair and hazel eyes; a young lady stands five foot six and has a beautiful facial glow; a young lady who's an African Native American Indian; a young lady who's mother was a African Zulu princess and whose father was a Native American Navaho Indian chief; a young lady who is a glamour model for magazine covers; a young lady who is a slavish fashion follower; a young lady who lives in Foot County, from the suburb of Dé Blur; a young lady who is the twelfth Heart of the Thirteen Hearts)

34. **Mrs. Shanty:** (A eighty-eight year old lady with bushy gray hair; a old lady who stands five foot two and has eyes grayish blue; a old lady who is a antique guru; a old lady who owns a antique shop called, Mrs. Old Shanty's Shack; a old lady who makes a low pitch eerie ear corking sound; a old lady who makes a low pitch eerie sound, "Hang, yang, yang, yi", when she really wants something; a old lady who lives in Foot County, from 900th Street in FallenForHer; a old lady who is friends of the Aitch sisters)

35. **Nick Gwil:** (A twenty eight year old man who has black hair and bowl cut; a man who stands five foot nine and has hazel eyes; a man who's skin pigment was tampered with to cause him to change to the color of sewage metallic green; a man who smells like a rotting carcass on the count of the chemical putrescine that's within his body was dabbled with; a man who is the fourth Greenfly of the Gangrene Gang; the laid back man; also known as D.A.M.N Green Flies)

36. **Noseboga:** (An unruly mythological creature; a creature half man and half serpent; a creature with four serpent headed limbs with an upper body of a human; a creature twenty foot long when stretched out, twelve to sixteen foot when moving about; a creature which lives in the center of the cloud that the kingdom of Sole once sat on; a blood thirsting creature; a creature that fights with large three pointed pitchforks; a

warrior of Princess Achlys; a anguipede with short frizzy white hair; the brother of Boganose; the anguipede that got plastered by a huge boulder)

37. **Okie Ka' Bokie:** (A twenty five year old young lady with long black hair; a young lady who stands five foot seven and has balloon blue color eyes; a young lady who is Japanese; a young lady who mastered of the martial arts and kickboxing world; a young lady who gets questioned, "Can you handle it", before a fight to get her fired up; a young lady who taught Aairrha and Sarah Breils to fight; a young lady who is a senryu writer; a young lady who lives in Foot County, from the suburb of Dé Blur; a young lady who is the sixth Heart of the Thirteen Hearts)

38. **Pete Stump:** (A twenty one year old young man who has thick curly red hair; a young man who stands five foot three and has eyes of hazel; a young man who has a two tune tough tarpon mug fisted full of freckles; a young man who has a generous heart like his sister Baby Doll; a young man with the nicknames of Pete N' Worm and Popcorn Pete; a young man who loves fishing; a young man who has a huge crush on Doodlebug; a young man from Foot County, from the suburb of Dé Blur)

39. **Podgy Littlewhich:** (A thirty five year old man with short black buzz cut hair; a man who stands five foot six; a man who's eyes changes colors to brown when it's cold and wet out, to hazel whenever its warm and hot out; a homely looking fellow; a fellow who is crime's own criminal; a man who gets judged on the way he looks and gets accused of, of things he never heard of; a man who gets made fun of; a man who is easy to take advantage of; a man who is a friend of the Aitch sisters)

40. **Prince Lowell:** (A prince from the kingdom of Sole; a prince who was to marry Princess Antoinette; a prince who was to rule the kingdom of Sole along side of Princess Antoinette; a prince who fought the anguipedes; a prince who fell from the cloud to his death from battling with a anguipede; a prince read about in the Book of Hearts)

41. **Prince Saul:** (An image of an infant held in the arms of Princess Antoinette; an infant held in a image for Princess

Antoinette to see; an image to show what the future could be; an image of an infant who could be the son of Princess Antoinette and Prince Lowell: an image casted by the stranger only to deceive; an image of an infant told about in the Book of Hearts)

42. **Princess Achlys:** (An unruly mythological creature; a female anguipede who is a princess; a creature half woman and half serpent; a creature with four serpent headed limbs with an upper body of a human; a creature twenty foot long when stretched out, twelve to sixteen foot when moving about; a creature which lives in the center of the cloud that the kingdom of Sole once sat on; a blood thirsting creature; an anguipede who wears a crown made up of hundreds of human jaw bones; an anguipede who wears a dress made up of tens of thousands of rattles of rattle snakes; an anguipede who carries a scepter made up of eight spine skulls woven together four on each end which can be pulled apart and used as weapons; an anguipede who battles Jenna Aitch)

43. **Princess Antoinette:** (A princess from the kingdom of Sole; a princess whose kingdom sat on a cloud; a princess who ruled a peaceful kingdom; a princess with eyes blue as the sky and long lushes soft hair white as snow; a princess who fought against the anguipedes; a princess whose prince was named Lowell; a princess read about in the Book of Hearts: a princess whose heart shaped gem is a diamond and wore the crown of clouds)

44. **Princess Athena:** (A princess that was read about in the Book of Hearts by Gina Aitch; a princess who was told about to Jenna and Doodlebug by Baby Doll Stump; a princess who's crown and heart shaped emerald gem were found but never placed on the Book of Hearts; a princess who's crown and emerald heart shaped gem is being held by Makenzie Drells)

45. **Princess Miranda:** (A princess told about by her younger sister Breanna who had escaped from the Book of Hearts; a princess who has yet to be read about)

46. **Ra-ra Rob:** (A fiend from hell that has a white afro; a fiend that stands a foot and a fourth tall; a fiend with yellow eyes and charcoal color skin; a fiend with cat like toenails and claws;

a fiend with shearing teeth; a fiend that hitched a ride out of hell on Makenzie's behind; a fiend that found a luxurious life while being spoiled by Makenzie; a fiend who only to Makenzie will listen)

47. **Regina Sumac:** (A twenty-five year old young lady, with long dark brown curly hair and eyes of hazel; a young lady who stands five foot five and is mildly complicated with freckles; a young lady from Country County and who has a master's degree in philosophy; a young lady who is the ninth Heart of the Thirteen Hearts; a young lady who is considered being the quiet one and the dork of the Thirteen Hearts)

48. **Roorin Tezory:** (A twenty year old young lady who has white hair dyed in the colors of a rainbow; a young lady who has albino eyes and pupils; a young lady who stands five foot three; a young lady who drives a Nessie ice cream truck throughout the neighborhoods in Foot County during the summer which is in the shape of the loch ness monster; an eccentric twenty year old young lady who dabbles in the supernatural; a young lady who has a masters degree in demonology; a young lady who is half Scottish and half Irish; a young lady who dresses as her heritage; a young lady who can find herself head deep in trouble before she knows it; a young lady who was in the same grade and classes as Doodlebug throughout her school years; a young lady who lives in Foot County, from an apartment in Foul Foot Street of FallenForHer; a young lady who's been lifelong friends with the Aitch sisters; a young lady who Doodlebug calls Rutabaga)

49. **Sal' Amanda:** (A woman of an unknown age who has long hair made of strands of black fire; a woman who stands six foot tall and has eyes of hell; a woman who is the darkness of hell; a woman who is without a soul; a woman who was awoken moments after Makenzie showed Gina the coffer; a woman who captured the robbed souls of the thirteen princesses that the stranger had stolen; a woman who created the Book of Hearts; a woman who is the Devil's daughter; a woman who's from hell)

50. **Salamander Sam:** (A ten inch long green purple spotted salamander; a salamander who loves Granny Jan's Crab Apple

Jam; a salamander who gets stuck in a sticky empty jar of raspberry jam; a salamander who gets freed by Walky and Talky; a salamander in a story written by Willard Wilson Drells)

51. **Samantha Buckles:** (A twenty three year old young lady with dark brown hair; a young lady who stands five foot four and has ocean blue eyes; a young lady with a devious pitchfork smile; a hectic young lady; a logorrhea young lady; a bolshie young lady; a young lady who's rambunctious; a young lady who's favorite thing to say is ludicrous; a young lady who owns and flies an air plane similar to the Red Barron's; a young lady who is a skywriter and barnstormer; a young lady who is rarely seen without her iron cross sunglasses; a young lady from What County; a young lady who is the eighth Heart of the Thirteen Hearts)

52. **Sarah Breils:** (A twenty-four year old young lady, with long dirty blond hair and deep sea blue eyes, who stands five foot five; a young lady who is a breeder of rare animals such as cassowary, babirusa hog, musk deer and giraffe neck antelope; a young lady who is a breeder of rare beetles such as rhinoceros and long jawed saw; a young lady who has the smarts in martial arts; a young lady who played for the Dé Blur Mimes during her high school years as number twelve and as a fullback; a young lady who lives in Foot County, from the suburb of Fallen; a young lady who is the second member of the Thirteen Hearts; a young lady who's the half sister to Aairrha Breils; a young lady who's a childhood friend of Makenzie)

53. **Seven Hairs:** (a twenty two year old lady who has long light brown hair; a young lady who stands five foot three and has eyes of hazel; a young lady who is a hunter of the big game; a young lady who had a masters degree in hoplology; a young lady who's fascinated with wars; a young lady who is fascinated with the rumors which came before wars; a young lady who owns a gun shop on E Street called, "Boom Chica Boom, Boom; young lady who's the girl friend of Burl; a young lady who lives in Foot County, from the suburb of Fallen; a young lady who is the seventh Heart of the Thirteen Hearts)

54. **Sophie Sofasock:** (A twenty one year old young lady with short black hair; a young lady who stands five foot five and has

navy-blue blue eyes; a young lady who lives in Greenground County; a young lady who played for the Greenground County Gators field hockey team during her high school years as number thirty five and as the center midfielder; a young lady who is a cousin of Marie W. Marry)

55. **Susan Sue Sousashoe:** (A twenty five year old young lady with long blond hair; a young lady who stands five foot six and has moonlit blue eyes; a young lady who is a horsewomen; a young lady who shows and has haute école; a young lady who is a horse breeder; a young lady who lives in Country County; a young lady who is the fifth Heart of the Thirteen Hearts)

56. **Talky:** (A seven inch tall white sock with two red stripes; a sock whose name was switched at birth; a sock that does more walking than talking; a sock who sets its self out with its brother Walky to help those in the need of help; a sock who helps Salamander Sam out; a sock in a story written by Willard Wilson Drells)

57. **The Devil:** (A ghoulish being who was kicked out of Heaven; the fallen angel; a evil being with threads of white hair that coils back on his nearly bowled scalp; a evil being with two horns, one at each side of his head with one being half broken; a evil being with yellow eyes and jagged rotten teeth; a evil being with a sinister smile and a voice like a dragon; a evil being with burnt blistery red wings and black brittle fingernails; a evil being who is shackled at the wrist with chains; a evil being whose home is hell; an evil being who Makenzie Drells and Gina Aitch had to go visit to get the key to unlock the coffer which held the Book of Hearts)

58. **The Faceless Witch of Hades:** (A evil being whose without a face but can see and hear very clearly; a evil being with long skeletal maggot infested yellowish white hair; a evil being with thick yellowish black six inch long fingernails; a hideous looking shag poke; a evil being who can trick one's mind with allusions; a evil being who is very powerful especially when in possession of the Book of Dark; a evil being who has yet to be told about in the Book of Hearts; a evil being who with the help of Makenzie Drells and Gina Aitch escaped from the

Book of Hearts; a evil being who is tied up in the cellar of Makenzie Drells house)

59. **The Stranger:** (A fiend who had escaped from Hell long ago; a fiend who was quite powerful but never knew how powerful; a fiend who turn his self into a human male; a fiend who had tricked the souls away from thirteen different princess; a fiend who had offspring by the thirteenth princess before her soul he took away; a fiend who's reign came to an end shortly after the fall of the thirteenth princess; a fiend who was taken back to Hell to burn not as his true self but as a living human male; a fiend who was transformed into a key which would unlock the coffer to unveil the Book of Hearts)

60. **Three headed panther:** (A mythological beast told about to Jenna and Doodlebug by Baby Doll Stump; a mythological beast which Baby Doll had to help fight off while helping Makenzie Drells to find the crown and emerald heart shaped gem of Princess Athena which the Thirteenth Heart Gina Aitch read about in the Book of Hearts)

61. **Topper:** (A thirty three year old man with short curly brown hair; a man who stands eight foot six and has brown eyes; a man who has a thick brown bushy beard and mustache; a man who was born and raised in Thule Greenland; a man who now lives in FallenForHer in a apartment in the Bullpen arena on Fallen Street; a man who is a wrestler for FallenForHer's Bullpen Wrestling origination; a man who is undefeated and is the heavy weight champion)

62. **Walky:** (A seven inch tall white sock with two blue stripes; a sock whose name was switched at birth; a sock that does more talking than walking; a sock who sets its self out with its brother Talky to help those in the need of help; a sock who helps Salamander Sam out; a sock in a story written by Willard Wilson Drells)

63. **Willard Wilson Drells:** (A five year old male child with thick dark brown hair; a male child stood little over three foot and had bluish green eyes; a male child who loved to doodle and write stories; a male child who wrote the story, "The Adventures of Walky and Talky; a male child who lost his life

in a car accident along with his parents; a male child who was the younger brother of Makenzie Drells)

64. **Xy:** (A nineteen year old young lady with straight long orange hair; a young lady who stands five foot four; a young lady who is deadly sexy and gorgeous; a young lady who has motley task for Hell's Hooligans the band she's in; a young lady who does backup vocals, plays backup guitar, plays keyboard, spits fire from her mouth, struts around; etcetera; a lady who is the devil of Hell's Hooligans; a young lady who wears a red leather devil outfit; a young lady who lives on the road she and her band travels on)